"Basher," I said, "I'm going to need some backup. Care to come along?"

"Where to?"

"Warehouses. Someone's putting the arm on the Vikk-shop Franchisees, shaking them down and making them sell bad merch."

Basher glowered at Teedo, who was calling for another round. "Anything to put a spike in *his* shoes."

I was about to leave when I saw something that stopped me cold. Devon Delrey came in, and right behind him were the two hardbodies who'd been following me around all day.

I nodded towards them. "Know who they are?"

Basher gave them a onceover. "Seen them on the Waterfront. They're off a ship from the south, one of Ishka Kunine's, I think."

"They were on my tail all day," I said. "I led them straight to the Assassin's Guild Hall."

ALSO BY ROBERTA ROGOW

THE SAGA OF HALVAR THE HIRELING

Murders in Manatas
Mayhem in Manata
Mischief in Manatas
Menace in Manatas
Malice in Manatas
Madness in Manatas

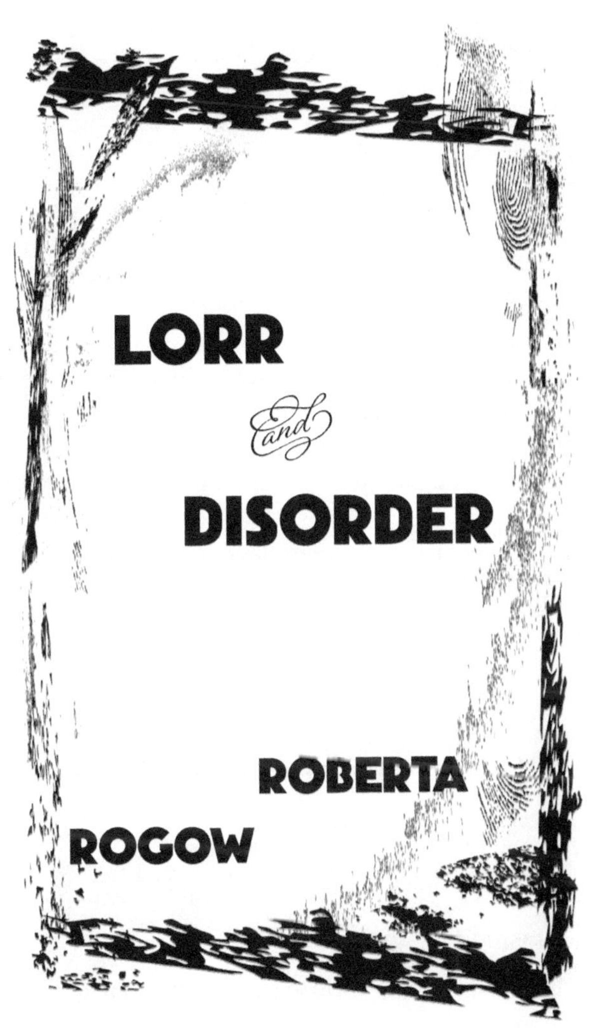

LORR

and

DISORDER

ROBERTA ROGOW

ZUMAYA OTHERWORLDS AUSTIN TX

2019

This book is a work of fiction. Names, characters, places and incidents are products of the author's imagination or are used fictitiously. Any resemblance to actual persons or events is purely coincidental.

"Zumaya Otherworlds" and the griffon colophon are trademarks of Zumaya Publications LLC, Austin TX
https://www.zumayapublications.com

Library of Congress Cataloging-in-Publication Data

Names: Rogow, Roberta, 1942- author.
Title: Lorr and disorder / by Roberta Rogow.
Description: Austin TX : Zumaya Otherworlds, 2019.
Identifiers: LCCN 2019019369 | ISBN 9781612714080 (softcover : acid-free
  paper) | ISBN 9781612714103 (epub)
Subjects: | GSAFD: Fantasy fiction.
Classification: LCC PS3568.O492 L67 2019 | DDC 813/.54--dc23
LC record available at https://lccn.loc.gov/2019019369

 DEDICATION

To John Betancourt and Carla Coupe, who invited me to play in their sandbox, and let me have it when they decided not to use it themselves.

A PRIVATE MATTER

"It's Unsanctioned, and I want it stopped!" Master Assassin Fee M'Farr stated firmly. He pounded on my desk for emphasis.

"I don't stop things," I reminded him. "I'm an Independent Eye. I watch and observe. I ask questions and make conclusions and report. That's what *I* do. What *you* do about it, that's *your* business. According to the Posts I saw last week, Marla Lily was found dead at the foot of the stairs in the house owned by Trader Drina Vikk. City Guard declared it a tragic accident. End of story."

I leaned back in my chair and observed Fee M'Farr. He doesn't look like an Assassin. He looks more like a successful grocer who's sampled more than a little of his own wares—round face, snub nose, good-size belly. That is, until you notice his eyes. They're the giveaway. They're like two chips of granite, gray and cold.

"Not according to the Dark One who took care of Lily," M'Farr said. "There are a few discrepancies in that report."

"Discrepancies?" A very big word for a very big lie. "Like what?"

"Like no bruises on the body, other than the one at the back of her neck that killed her." He shifted in the wooden chair I keep for my clients—unpadded, and not very comfortable to sit in. I don't want my clients to wait around and chat. Tell me what you want me to do, then let me do it. That's how Pola Drach does business, and I've been doing it long enough to get a good rep. You want an Eye, you come to Drach.

Of course, the Guilds have their own people to investigate Guild problems, but there are some things folks don't want the Guild to mess with—family matters like who's cheating on who, or who's dipping into the family coffers. In that case, there aren't too many options. There's The Brain, but she's too higher-up to handle little things like straying spouses. And there's Basher Bob, if you need muscle. I do the job clean and quiet, and I don't make a lot of fuss about it.

I looked M'Farr over again. "And you know this how?"

"Any time there's a death that's not absolutely due to bad health, I want to know about it," he admitted. "I make a nice donation to the Temple every month to ensure the Dark Ones keep me informed. Something like this happens, it's bad for business." He'd said the forbidden word aloud. No one else in Lorr would speak so casually about loss of life.

"I see," I said. "If word got out that someone actually got murdered without the help of the Fatsos, then people might start wondering what they're paying you protection for. That would definitely hurt your bottom line." I could be just as crass as he was.

M'Farr glared at the reference to the Honorable Guild of Forgers, Assassins, Thieves. and Swindlers as rendered by the common folk of Lorr.

"You've got a smart mouth, Drach," he gritted out.

"I know," I said, with my blandest bland smile. "I also know there's more to this than you're telling me. But a job's a job, and the Guild is good for it. I charge a silver a day, plus expenses."

"Here's three silvers. That'll cover you for three days." He laid out the coin. "And I'll want a tally of those expenses when you're done."

"Am I working for the Guild or for you?" I asked as I reached into the desk for my standard form. I like to get it down in writing. It saves the fee of an advocate if the client isn't happy with what I find out when I'm Eyeing.

M'Farr shifted in the chair again.

"You're working for me, personally," he said. "This is a private matter. I don't want the Guild in on it. Not yet, anyway. If it turns out this is about some amateur trying to save a bit or two, I'll take care of it. If it's a pro, then it becomes something for the Guild to handle."

"I'll still need a badge," I reminded him. As an Independent, I don't carry one.

M'Farr reached into a jacket pocket and came up with a round token with the Guild's Sigil on it—a sword crossed with a pen.

"How far do I dig?"

I may not have access to the Big Black Box that holds all the Admin records, but I can go pretty far. I have a few resources the City Guard can't use, even if they wanted to.

"Just find out who did it, and leave the rest to me," M'Farr ordered.

I handed him the form, he signed, and he was out the door into Clothiers Alley, mingling with the rest of the shoppers, just another citizen going about his business. After all, business is what Lorr is all about, and mine is just another service industry.

I leaned back in my chair and thought for all of two minutes about whether I was doing the right thing, getting mixed up in a Fatso Guild matter. Then I scooped up the coin. I have rent to pay on the office, small as it is—one room in Clothier's Alley behind the choicest boutique in Lorr. I also have to pay rent on my digs on Entertainment Row, I have my food bill at Fletcher's, and there's the fresh potting soil for Ficus. M'Farr's coin is as good as anyone else's.

ii

So, off to work. No one better than a clothier to tell you the real dirt about the Upper Tier. I strolled around the corner to Jake and Holly's, my landlords and the top-flight dressmakers in Lorr, to see what they had to say about the Vikk clan and Marla Lily's connection to them. They owe me a favor or two since I got the goods on a little pin-holder who was pinching their best designs and peddling them to their chief rivals down the Grand Boulevard. Last I heard, the kid was running a loom some-

4

where in the southlands near Pangkot, Jake's designs were safe, and Holly could charge top coin for an exclusive.

Jake waved me off as soon as I mentioned the name Drina Vikk.

"Don't talk to us about that old miser! She's the one behind the Vikk-shops. Ruining business! Undercutting the Merchants' Guild! She even sells clothing without the sanction of the Clothier's Guild!"

"And she's never bought another dress since her Dearly Beloved Olber passed to Eternal Rest twenty years ago," Holly added bitterly. "Not from us, not from anyone. She just remakes her old ones, over and over. And her daughter Kaisrin, the one who's espoused to Devon Delrey, doesn't come to us, either. She prefers that dowd Gieranch." She made a face to express what she thought of her rival's designs.

"What about this Marla Lily? Clothier's model?" I looked around their shop, They didn't seem to lack for customers. Two stout women fingered skirts displayed on a bench, and two slimmer ones watched as a very slender young beauty pirouetted before them, exhibiting a sheer blouse that didn't quite reveal what was underneath.

"She said she was," Jake said slowly. "She worked for us, and sometimes took a job showing goods at private parties. Word was, she was looking for a patron and moved in on Teedo Vikk." He nodded meaningfully.

I nodded back. I've seen Teedo around in the bars and Licensed Houses. He's known as a player, likes a good time when his mother lets him have the coin.

"How'd they meet?" Considering that Elder Vikk wasn't shopping at Jake and Holly's, and daughter preferred elsewhere, it would seem that Marla and Teedo weren't exactly fated to connect.

"Like I said, Marla got hired by some of our colleagues to show their new styles," Jake said. "There are private parties where the new clothes are displayed. Teedo likes to go to them, to see what's new—not the clothes, the ones wearing them. For instance, Selva Delrey is one of our top clients. She had Marla display our designs at one of her little gatherings. Good sales for us, and a new patron for Marla."

"And we don't mean Selva," Holly added. "Elder Vikk may be a straightlaced Conservationist, but Teedo's not."

"So, Teedo meets Marla," I summed up, "Teedo takes up with her. Why take her home to meet Mam?"

"No idea," Holly said with a dismissive shrug. "Once she landed Teedo, Marla Lily was gone from Clothier's Alley. That was about three weeks ago. I suppose she thought she'd landed the big fish."

"She landed *something*," I said. "Thanks for the input, friends."

Holly looked me over. "You know, Pola, you need to brighten yourself up. We've got a new line from the weavers in Flatlands, some kind of new wool their boffins came up with, and a new dye, too. It would match your skin perfectly. Honey-gold, made up in a slim skirt, a fitted jacket. It would show off the curves..."

She stopped, warned by my frown. I don't want to be noticed. I've got a whole wardrobe full of drab dresses, tatty skirts, blouses with lace that's just a touch dingy. When I'm not pretending to be an office drone, I prefer trou to skirts—easier to get around in, and better if I have to do rough work, although, to be honest, I try to stay away from that. My usual work depends on my fitting into the crowd.

When you look at me, you see a slightly dumpy, not-quite-middle-aged female with honey-gold skin and green eyes, just like any of hundreds you'll see in Lorr toting their groceries home from market, scribbling away in offices, running small shops, and taking care of children while parents are scribbling in offices and running small shops. Oh, I can dress up for an occasion, but most of the time, an Eye has to be invisible. An unattractive female is as good as invisible in Lorr, and that's the way I like it.

"I'll think about it," I told Holly. I might buy the outfit, but not today. Once in a while, I have to put on a show. A new suit might come in useful, and if this assignment worked out, I'd have the coin for it.

iii

Next stop was more difficult. I had my token from the Guild, but that might not be enough to get me into the Dark Ones' Temple. I spent a bit on a carrier-ride to the end of the line, then had a goodly walk to the Final Shrine halfway up Dark One's Hill, where the bodies of the deceased are kept before disposal.

It's a stark box of a building—no curlicues or paint, just the bricks and blocks and a simple red-and-white sign over the front door. No one likes to think about what's inside a Dark One's Temple. Death is the great evil, the one thing in Lorr that's never spoken of, to be avoided at all costs. Dark Ones deal with it every day, one way or another; and it marks them, inside and out, more than the dark-blue robes and plain blue trou and jackets they wear.

I got the usual guff from the Dark One at the door when I asked for an interview with the Medico who'd written the report on Marla Lily, but in the end, the token got me ten minutes with a smug, supercilious long noodle named Eldo Kelvin in a bare cell of a room that reeked of what they douse the bodies in before they take them to the Burning Pits—a sickly-sweet soapy smell mixed with the musk of incense from the Temple. No chairs, not even a bench to sit on. Just him, and me, and four walls, ceiling, and floor.

He strode in, long robe flapping, long nose sniffing, set of lenses perched atop said nose, long hair flying in all directions.

"If you are here to question my findings in the matter of Marla Lily, then let me remind you I am a qualified Medico," he snapped before I had a chance to say a word.

"And just what *were* those findings?" I snapped back. "Where's this report?"

"I turned it over to the City Guard," he said haughtily. "As per routine. And they ignored it. Ignored it!" he repeated, radiating indignation. How dare a mere City Guard ignore the report of a qualified Dark One!

"Post said the death was accidental," I said.

"Pah!" Kelvin glared at me through his lenses. "I am not blind. If I say there were no bruises on the body, there *were* none. That woman did not fall down those stairs. She was placed at the bottom of them deliberately. I noted the lividity of the limbs, the placement of blood engorgement…"

"Cause?" I did not utter the forbidden word.

"A blow to the back of the neck that severed the spinal cord…here." He pointed to the back of his own neck.

"With what?"

"That is difficult to say. There were no characteristic marks of any particular blunt instrument, such as a cane or club. A very strong person could have done it with a hand, of course. I have seen demonstrations of the skill."

So have I, and it's a specialized one. It's part of Guards training, hand-to-hand combat for use in restraining obstreperous prisoners. Most folks don't bother with that kind of skill. The average citizen of Lorr depends on a stout cudgel for self-defense. I usually carry a small one myself, just in case I run into something unexpected while I'm Eyeing.

"Medico Dark Kelvin, please tell me exactly how and why you were called to the Vikk house." I laid it on thick, giving him his full title.

"And who desires this information?"

"I ask on behalf of Master Assassin Fee M'Farr. He's hired me to make sure Marla Lily's demise was, indeed, accidental."

Kelvin sniffed at me, but that might have been his reaction to the ever-present deadhouse reek of rotting meat and incense.

"It was my turn on the rotation for night duty," he said. "A message was sent from Striver's Hill guardhouse via comm. They had been summoned to the house of Master Merchant Drina Vikk. There had been an accidental death in the house. The family servant demanded that the body should be removed as quickly as possible.

"I took the skimmer to said house, where I was let in by said servant, who provided me with the ritual basin for washing.

"I was then shown the body of a young woman dressed in an evening gown, lying at the foot of a long flight of stairs. The servant informed me this was a Marla Lily, a guest in the house, and that she had fallen down the stairs in the night."

"And you didn't accept this?"

"I do not accept hearsay evidence," Kelvin said. "I make my own conclusions. I turned the body over and examined it carefully."

"And you concluded…?"

"As I stated in my official report, the woman was killed by a blow to the back of the neck. How many times must I repeat this? I have work to do, I cannot stand here and waste time!"

"Conservationist, are you?" I commented.

"My beliefs are not under discussion, Eye Drach. I sent my report to the City Guards and they ignored it. I also sent a copy to Master Assassin M'far."

"Who pays you to keep him informed," I summed up. "Well, Kelvin, he's paying me to do the same. Is there anything else you may have noticed? Something inconsequential you didn't put in your report? For instance, what was the manner of the chief servant towards you?"

Kelvin had been about to leave, but stopped in his tracks. "His manner?"

"Was he upset? Did he look pleased, unhappy, distressed?" I pressed him. Dark Ones don't usually notice anyone or anything around them, but I was taking a chance this one might have something for me that wasn't in the reports.

Kelvin looked blankly back at me. "He was a servant, dressed in a servant's livery. He held the basin with both hands..." He paused. "It nearly slipped out of his hands," he said thoughtfully. "The servant's hands were wet."

"Odd," I said. "He wasn't the dishwasher, was he?"

"The chief servant, as I said. He behaved as though it was granting an honor he should lead me into house, even for such a distressing errand as mine."

"And you didn't speak to anyone else? None of the family came to observe the body?"

Kelvin sniffed again. "Hardly, Eye Drach. Only we Dark Ones are allowed into the presence of the Dead, and even we must wash before and after touching them."

"That's what I thought."

"And one more thing," Kelvin added. "My observations are very thorough." He cleared his throat, meaningfully. "I had to cut."

"Oh?" I didn't like the sound of that.

"The female was with child," he said.

"That wasn't in the report," I pointed out.

"It was not pertinent to her decease," Kelvin said sniffily. "She would have had the child in six months had she not been killed."

That put a new face on things.

"Medico Dark Kelvin, I thank you for your very valuable time, and I hope you have a pleasant day."

He didn't bother to return the wish. He strode off, robe and hair flapping. I decided not to bother looking at the late Marla Lily. Doing so wasn't going to give me any more than what Kelvin already had, which was enough to make me wonder just who in the House of Vikk *didn't* want Marla Lily dead.

iv

There was one more stop to make before I actually tackled the House of Vikk—the touchiest of the day.

I have a spotty relationship with the City Guard. On the one hand, I spent a year in the Guard, so in one sense, I'm one of them. On the other, my term ended badly, with recriminations on both sides. I happened to see something I wasn't supposed to, and I reported it to my superiors, the way I was supposed to; and I found out that there are times when it's better not to speak up.

For once, the Founders were with me. I got to the Guard House at the base of Admin Hill at turn-of-shift, and nailed Captain Sara Atterson as she was heading out the gates of the compound into the plaza. She had told me not to present my findings to our superior officer. Now, she's a captain, and I'm on my own. That's the way it goes in Lorr.

12

"Oyo, Captain Atterson! How's business? Got time for a brew?"

"Eye Drach, I always have time for a brew, but not always with you. What do you want?" Atterson didn't even break her stride, heading for one of the stands that sold clet, snacks, and brew to the guards.

"Can't I have a sit-down with an old friend?" I steered her to the nearest food stall. "Brew or clet?"

"I'm not an old friend. We spent a term together before you were canned, and I don't have any information for you," Atterson snapped. "And I'm not ready for brew. Clet for me."

She accepted the mug offered to her. I loathe clet, can't even stand the smell of it. I got a mug of brew.

"What kind of information would I need from you?" I hefted my mug and took a sip. Not bad stuff, for roadside brew. "And why do you think I want it?"

"The Guard on patrol in Shopper's Row spotted Master Assassin Fee M'Far in Clothiers Alley," Atterson stated. "M'Far doesn't buy from Jake and Holly, and doesn't need anything from the Clothiers Guild. Guard Gilles is an eager young sprout who takes his job seriously. When he sees something or someone strange on his beat, he reports it immediately to his superior, who just happens to be me.

"So I start to think. What has happened recently that would send M'Far into a snit? And I think about that female found dead up on Striver's Hill, and I think maybe someone's poaching on Guild territory, and Master Assassin M'far wants to find out more, but on the quiet. You have an office in Clothier's Alley, behind Jake and Holly's Boutique. So, you are looking into the passing of Marla Lily. Like the Math Master at the Academy used to say, 'That's been shown'."

"Better rein the kid in, then," I said. "If he reports everything he sees when he's on patrol, he might see something he shouldn't. He might wind up like me, an Independent Eye." I took another sip of brew, and let it go at that. No use getting muzzy this early in the day. "Who took the call on Marla Lily?"

"Striver's Hill Patrol," Atterson said with a shrug.

I knew what that shrug meant. The City Guard isn't paid all that much. The householders on Striver's Hill don't want to shell out for extra protection from the Fatso Guild, so they pay the local patrol to step up their watches.

"What do *you* think?" I asked.

Another shrug.

"Not my affair," Atterson said. "Guard Master says it's an accident, Master Merchant Drina Vikk says it's an accident, it goes down in the records as an accident, unless someone comes up with something better."

"And if someone does?"

"The case is closed." Atterson slammed down her mug. "It's a private matter, Drach. Don't interfere with Guard business."

"It's Fatso Guild business now," I reminded her. "Anything useful I should know about the Vikks?"

"Only that Master Merchant Drina Vikk is a nasty piece of work, and you'd better watch your step with her, Eye Drach. And Merchant Teedo has an eye for the ladies—"

"That I know," I said. "And Commander Affrey Vikk is the pride of the Aerial Corps. Elder sister Kaisrin is linked into the Delrey clan, who run most of the money that goes in and out of Lorr. Anyone else?"

"The youngest, Betriz, is said to be champing at the bit to take over from Elder Vikk, but it's the mam who runs the business, and she isn't about to let go. And that's all I can tell you, Pola Drach. Thanks for the clet."

And off she went, swaggering down the road, leaving me with the bill and two empty mugs.

So, now I knew a little bit more than I had before about the Vikks, but that didn't help get me into the Vikk house.

I headed over to the News Posts in front of the Central Guard House to see if there was anything I should know before I tackled Striver's Hill. Post One had a notice about volcanoes up north disrupting weather conditions, and a statement from the Autocrat of Pangkot protesting imposts on goods coming from the south. Post Two had an announcement about a new Council appointment, and a rehash of the eternal conflict between the Craftsmen's Guild and the Merchants. There was a crowd around Post Three checking the latest figures from the Bankers' Guild on the money market, and another around Post Four commenting on the judgment of a certain music critic, who was being snarky about the latest singer at the Opera. I skipped Post Five—I don't bet on the races, and watching two bruisers whack each other bloody isn't my idea of fun.

That left Post Six, the one that holds the gossip-sheets, and where people leave anonymous hints as to evil-doings amongst the highborn with low tastes.

What I found were a lot of scurrilous rumors about various Guild-Masters and their expensive habits, who was seen at this or that Licensed House of Pleasure, and one tidbit buried under two or three other tidbits asking "Has the sudden friendship between two brothers-in-law ripened or soured because of their mutual interest in a Clothier's model?"

That gave me something to consider as I made my way across Lorr to Striver's Hill.

v

I thought that last bit of gossip over on the carrier-ride across town to Striver's Hill, the district where the Vikk clan had established itself some twenty years before when Olber Vikk took residence in a house built by a formerly wealthy merchant who'd had the bad luck to lose his fortune to pirates.

You can tell who's up and who's down by their position on Striver's Hill. The Delrey house is right at the top, a grand mansion that towers over the rest of them, as befits the most prestigious bankers in Lorr. The Vikk house is midway down the hill. I can't tell whether it's grand or not. It's surrounded by a wall—concrete plastered over brick, topped with spikes, penetrated by two gates. One is an elaborate wrought-iron masterpiece with an entwined D/O monogram—for Drina and Ol-

16

ber—meant for invited guests and other gentry. Farther along the wall is a plain wooden door marked "Deliveries", which does for the rest of us.

Striver's Hill is not a good place for Eyeing. I couldn't find a likely nook in the blank face of wall that separated the houses on either side of the curving road. There were no handy food stalls to lounge at, no peddlers to chat up, not even a tree to lean against. No one walks up Striver's Hill casually. There was a country-looking fellow with a handcart delivering foodstuffs to one or another of those hidden houses making his way down the hill, but I was the only other person in sight. Even the servants hid behind the walls.

To make the point clearer, along came one of those pesky Guard patrols—one fresh-faced young recruit, one hardened vet.

"Are you lost, Friend?" the younger Guard asked politely while the older one gave me the onceover, trying to peg my status.

I have prepared a good excuse for just such an occasions.

"I was sent by my Guild to deliver a message to the Merchant Bruno residence, but I must have taken a wrong turning," I said.

"Not on this street," the younger Guard told me curtly. "Go down the hill, around, and up the other side."

"Take care, woman," the older Guard added.

"I'll do that. Thank you, Guardsmen." At least, *I* had been polite. Maybe I looked out-of-place on Strivers' Hill, but he didn't have to be nasty about it.

I headed back down the hill while they watched to make sure I did. It was a long, hot slog, and I decided I couldn't take a chance I'd be nailed Eyeing. I'd have to get into the Vikk house somehow, but doing it would take a little time.

It was getting towards sundown, and I wanted to learn a bit more about the Vikk-Delrey connection before I tackled Drina Vikk. It's always better to know more than your adversary thinks you do.

vi

I headed for Entertainment Row and my digs. I stopped at the one of the market-carts along the way to pick up a round of cheese and a small loaf of sweet bread for my evening snack. Fletcher's Food Shop provides most of my meals, but Fletcher closes his ovens after the Silver Moon sets, and I sometimes get hungry waiting for him to open in the morning.

I have two rooms—a bedroom that faces the inner yard where the loo and wash-house are, and a sitting room that faces the street, furnished with a table where I can have my meals, a large chair with an alcohol lamp where I can read and write my reports, and a stand for Ficus near the window so it can observe the street below. Once in a while I open the window and let Ficus get a chance at pollination, but I don't really want Ficus to pollinate. I know that, once pollinated, Ficus will produce one seed, then die.

Some of the Conservationists will argue that I'm keeping Ficus from completing its appointed mission, and I admit it—I'm being selfish. I want to keep Ficus with me for as long as I can. It's something alive in my life, and there are the added benefits, which I prefer to keep to my-self.

I smelled the warning it projected before I opened the door. I had my cudgel in my hand when I entered.

Master Assassin Fee M'Farr sat at my table, reading my private report-book. I didn't bother with a "How's business?"

"What are you doing here?" I yelled. "How did you find this place?"

M'Farr grinned nastily. "I'm an Assassin, remember? Just because I don't do it now doesn't mean I can't. I was trained by Master Kudos himself."

I wasn't impressed. "I don't care if you were trained by the Founders of Great Memory. This is my home, and you are invading it. What do you want?"

"I want to know why you're not at the Vikk house," M'Farr snapped.

"Do you want me to do this job or not?" I shot back. "I'm a professional. I do the job the way I think it should be done. If you didn't want me to do it, you should have let one of your own people investigate. You've got plen-ty of spies on your payroll."

"I told you, this is a private matter. I don't want the Guild involved, not yet."

"Then let me do what you're paying me to do."

M'Farr grimaced. "You're wasting my money, buy-ing clet for the Guards."

I made an exasperated noise. "You and the Guards Patrol should get together on this. One of their rookies spotted you in Clothier's Alley. Now you tell me one of the Fatsos spotted me with my Guards contact."

"Don't call the Guild that!" M'Farr's face grew red with indignation. "We're the Honorable Guild of Forgers, Assassins, Thieves, and Swindlers, and don't you forget it! And I expect a little more action than I'm getting right now."

"Eyeing isn't active," I told him. "What I'm doing now is mostly thinking, and what I'm thinking is that I'm going to have to find another set of digs if this one is known. There are a few people out there who may not appreciate what I've found out about them and will take it out on me. They may even try to uproot Ficus, and that would really make me unhappy." I didn't elaborate. I also didn't tell him that Ficus isn't exactly defenseless.

M'Farr got up from the table. "What are you going to do now?"

I put down my net bag with the bread and cheese.

"I'm going to water Ficus. I'm going downstairs to Fletcher's for my dinner. I'm going to make the rounds of the bars and brothels, chat up a few people, and see what I can find out about Marla Lily that might make someone want to kill her. And maybe tomorrow, when I've got my facts straight, I'll try to get into the Vikk house. If I'm really lucky, I'll have a word with Master Merchant Drina Vikk."

"And then what?" Fee needled me.

I didn't rise to his bait. "And then, I'll tell you what I find out, and what I conclude. Come to my office tomorrow at sundown. And don't come here again!"

"I'm an Assassin, Drach. I go where I want to go." Before I could stop him, he went through my bedroom, out the window into the yard, and disappeared into the growing dusk.

"I guess an Assassin isn't going to go in and out the front door," I told Ficus while I put the bread and cheese into the cold-box under the washbasin and sluiced the day's grime off my face and neck. I dabbed some water on Ficus's leaves, too. "You'll be all right. I don't think Fee M'Farr is going to send anyone to uproot you. At least, not tonight."

vii

I decided to dress for a night of bar-hopping in an almost-new black wool jacket trimmed with steel beads on the collar and cuffs, worn over a red linen shirt, and black wool trou. I hooked the gopherwood truncheon on my trouser-belt, popped my best flip-brim felt hat onto my head, and began my rounds with Fletcher's and a hearty meal of roast beast, root-veg, brew, and local gossip.

Then it was down Entertainment Row, where the most popular bars were doing their usual best to separate rich people from their coin. It was all routine for a summer night in Lorr. Entertainers, Licensees, Beggars, and Thieves were out in force, assisting in the distribution of wealth, as the Education Masters at the Academy put it. Reps from most of the better Guilds were out for a night's fun and games, badges on display so folks could tell who was who and act accordingly. Merchants, Seamen, Clothiers, Craftsmen, Grocers—even a gang of giggling Mothers, away from the kiddies for an evening—all mingling by the light of the colored lanterns that swung overhead

21

in the breeze wafting from the estuary at the mouth of the river, cooling the air from too hot to pleasantly warm. I spotted the Guards, keeping things calm, getting between a couple of young Aerial Corps jokers and some Beggars who were a little too persistent.

I checked in with some of the Licensees, but no one wanted to discuss Marla Lily. It's not a good idea to think about the deceased, especially the ones who meet their end by violence.

I headed down towards the bridge that leads across the river to Flatlands, where most of the mechs, techs, and office drones make their homes. The bridge entry marks the boundary between the respectable parts of Lorr and the Waterfront. The carrier rails end at the bridge, and the docks begin there. The company wasn't select—fewer Guild badges on view, more Thieves and Beggars, and a lot more Aerial Corps, spending their pay. The Licensees aren't classy, the Entertainers were more raucous, and the brew is pure river-sludge.

At the end of the row is the most notorious of the Waterfront District taverns. Smokey Joe's is a long, low building with a blank facade, sprawled alongside the river.

I nodded to the doorkeeper, Sneaky Pete, when I entered. He nodded back. Pete and I have long acquaintance, no problems with me. I don't start trouble, and I prefer not to take part in any rough stuff that may go down if someone else starts it.

The noise and smell battered my sensory nerves as soon as I entered. I checked out the clientele and spotted the one person I hoped would be there.

Basher Bob, a big dark-skinned dude in black leather jacket and heavy trou, was sitting at the bar with his favorite female, a red-headed popsy called Velda,

"Oyo, Drach." He lifted his glass in greeting. "How's business? I hear you're on the Vikk case."

"Now, who told you that?" I asked, accepting a brew from Barkeep Joe. He knew my tastes, always had a mug for me. I stay away from jack, especially the kind you find at Smokey Joe's. I think they distill it from sundew pods.

"Word gets out." He winked at me. "Take a word from someone who knows, Drach. Stay clear of the Vikks."

"Got you good, did they?" I took a cautious sip of the brew. Smokey Joe's varies, depending on whose batch is on tap.

"Something hinky going down," Basher said with a meaningful look at the far corner. "I keep out of stuff like that."

"Unless you're paid in gold," I muttered.

I looked casually around and saw what he meant. Two gents not of a sort likely to be seen in Smokey's sat at a table trying to look like they belonged. In full dress, with toppers? Not on your Nellie Bly!

One was a portly type, red-faced and piggy-eyed, with a growing tum. The other could only be called "A Gentleman of Distinction"—elegant, slender, and carefully groomed, with a head of pale hair and a harried expression, as if he wondered whether his purse was safe.

Well, well, well, I said to myself. *Teedo Vikk and Devon Delrey. What are you doing in a place like this?*

Devon got up and left, and Teedo beckoned to one of the Licensees posing at the bar. I didn't think much of his taste—she wasn't especially young or pretty, but then, by the time they got to working at Smokey's they wouldn't be. He made his negotiations, and the two of them headed to her crib just as Barkeep Joe let out a yell.

"What the...? What's with this coin?" he yelped.

"What's wrong with it?" Manager Joe, a skinny rat-faced specimen in a well-worn dress suit, came out of his cubbyhole of an office, where he sits and watches the action.

"It's supposed to be a silver, but it's going blank!"

Everyone in the bar crowded around the barkeep and watched as the coin in his hand lost its shine and went dull, turning from a Silver to a Bit in a minute or two.

"Where'd you get this?" Manager Joe frowned down at the coin.

"I don't know, it was in the till with the rest of the take."

Manager Joe's frown turned into a ferocious scowl. "Every coin gets tested," he ordered. "And this goes to the Council tomorrow!"

I finished my brew and headed back to my digs. Both Gold Moon and Silver Moon had set, and mist was rising from the river. The bridge was ahead, but no one was near it. The carrier transporters had left for the night; the guards were out on patrol.

I forgot the first rule of Eyeing: be ever watchful. Instead, I was thinking about what I'd seen and heard during the day.

Then I got a whiff of something I knew wasn't river water—more like the kind of soap used for hard scrubbing, with a dash of incense musk. I whirled around, swinging my truncheon, just in time to avoid a *whap* on the back of my neck. The truncheon connected, and I heard a satisfying smack as wood hit flesh. There was a yell and the sound of retreating footsteps.

I peered through the growing river-fog, but all I could make out was a dim form that disappeared into the mist. Someone had just made a big mistake. When someone tries to stop me from Eyeing, I know I'm getting close. I just wasn't sure what I was getting close to!

viii

I didn't waste too much time next morning on the usual stuff—slosh some water over the face and tip the excess into Ficus's pot, comb the hair into some kind of order, pick out a respectable-looking outfit for a visit to the Vikk mansion. I chose a nice, neat gray set— trou and jacket, lapels picked out with silver embroidery, pale ivory lace-trimmed shirt underneath. No truncheon today, just my sapper in the jacket pocket in case someone got too friendly. Black flip-brim, and I was ready for work. I don't use facepaint—don't need it or want it. Business-like, that was the effect I wanted.

I took the carrier back to Striver's Hill, hoping not to run into those Guards from the day before. This time around I rang the front gate bell, like I belonged there.

It was answered by a geezer in old-style livery, a black tailcoat the likes of which hasn't been seen in Lorr since the Merchant's War twenty years ago. He looked me up and down through the bars of the iron gate and demanded, "What do you want here?"

"I want to speak to Master Merchant Drina Vikk," I said. "I have a message from Master Assassin Fee M'Farr."

"We do not do business with Master Assassins," the geezer said.

"Master Assassin M'Farr thinks differently," I told him, showing my badge. "And he has sent me to ask some questions about the demise of Marla Lily."

"That was an accident," the geezer insisted. "There are no questions. It has been decided, and the matter is closed." He tried to do the same to the gate.

"There are still questions to be asked," I stated. "And if I don't ask them, I'll have to take the word back to Master Assassin M'Farr that I was denied entry. And that would be—unfortunate."

I let him think that over for a while.

Behind me, I heard the squeak of wheels. A pedishaw tooled up, drawn by a stout fellow in a red uniform, carrying a woman in the most stylish of morning dresses. The geezer opened the gate to let her inside, and I took advantage of the opportunity to follow her in before he could close it.

I found myself in a paved courtyard, flagstones with a tidy border of bricks. The house was in the form of an open square, the wall forming one side, and a central core flanked by two wings the rest. A set of shallow steps led up to a carved wooden door, just ajar, where I could see a female servant carrying something from one room to another.

"Now, Servant, I want to speak with Master Merchant Drina Vikk," I repeated, more forcefully..

The passenger in the pedishaw stepped down and looked me over. She was a little older than me, tall and angular, with a sour expression that spoiled her otherwise pretty face.

"Why do you wish to speak with my mam?" she asked.

This must be Kaisrin Vikk, espoused to Devon Delrey. I wondered if she knew where her spouse was last night?

Aloud, I said, "Master Assassin M'Farr is upset that an unfortunate incident occurred in a house that was under his protection. He sent me to reassure Master Merchant Vikk it wasn't done with his approval, and it won't happen again."

I smiled ingratiatingly, laying it on thick. "He is grateful for the donations Master Merchant Vikk makes to the honorable Assassins' Guild, and he is taking steps to see that her franchisees are not inconvenienced by unsanctioned thieves."

"Follow me." Kaisrin led me up the walk to the front door. The servant tried to protest, but she snapped, "Baroney, I will take this person to see my mam. You do not have to be present."

"I'm always present," Baroney said, and he followed us into the house.

I took a gander at the surroundings—a large hall, raised roof, lots of wood paneling, paintings of people long dead and gone, including a lifesize portrait of the late Olber Vikk in his full Merchant's Guild regalia, looking as if he'd just swallowed a sour fruit.

The hall floor was set with black and white slabs of stone. One spot looked slightly brighter than the rest, right at the foot of the staircase.

"Is that where it happened?" I asked, nodding at the clean spot on the floor.

Kaisrin gave me a look as if to say *Ghoulish person, to mention the Dead!* Aloud, she said, "That is where the unfortunate Marla Lily was found."

"Who found her?" I asked.

"I did," Baroney spoke up. "I heard a noise and came to see what was happening. She was lying right there. She was…gone."

"How did you know that? You didn't, um, touch her, did you?"

Kaisrin let out a squawk of disgust. "One does not do such things!" Now she *really* had me pegged as a lowlife.

"I see the spot's been scrubbed," I observed.

"I did that once the unfortunate remains were removed," Baroney said.

A door at one side of the staircase opened, and a female emerged. *This must be Betriz*, I thought. She was about ten years younger than me, a shorter, paler version of Kaisrin, dressed in the outfit worn by office drones and senior Academy students—dark skirt, white cotton shirtwaist with a lace collar, hair braided and coiled up out of the way.

"This person is here to see Mam," Kaisrin explained. "From the Guild." She didn't have to say which Guild—the Fatsos are the only one that doesn't make a big deal about what they really do.

"Mam isn't seeing anyone," Betriz reported.

"She'll see me," I said firmly. "Master Assassin Fee M'Farr sent me. *Personally*," I added.

"I will ask her, then." Betriz let her sister pass through the door, leaving me alone with Baroney.

We eyed each other, sizing each other up. I pegged him as one of the old-style servants, almost part of the family. He had me down as an underling, not worth the time to talk to.

"This is where it happened," I repeated after a minute or two of uncomfortable silence.

"Yes." He wasn't going to waste words on me.

"How did she come to fall?"

"I couldn't say."

I persisted with the questions, whether he'd answer them or not.

"Was she going up the stairs? Down? What was she doing upstairs anyway? Isn't that where the sleeping-rooms are?"

"Master Merchant Drina Vikk's private quarters are directly above us," Baroney admitted. "Merchant Teedo Vikk has a suite in the South Wing." He pointed to the side of the house that would get the most sunlight. "Junior Merchant Betriz has rooms upstairs."

"Was Marla Lily heading for Teedo's private suite?" I asked, with a wink and a leer.

"That is not for me to say." But his face said it, all right, and he didn't approve, not one bit.

"Servant Baroney," I began again, "please think back to the night that Marla Lily suffered her accident. Was there anything unusual? A quarrel, for instance?"

"There was a family dinner," Baroney said at last. "Merchant Teedo announced that he and the female known as Marla Lily were about to formalize their union."

"That must have pleased his mother," I said, with another wink.

"That creature did not belong here," Baroney said fiercely. "She was wastefully extravagant. She asked for more food at dinner!"

"Did she?" Considering Master Merchant Drina Vikk's reputation for thrift, that's not surprising. Teedo didn't get his bulk at Mam's table, that was for sure!

"Merchant Teedo should not have brought her here," Baroney said.

"She was going to be part of the family," I reminded him.

"That would not happen!" Baroney snapped, just as the door reopened.

"Master Merchant Drina Vikk will see you now," Kaisrin announced.

I walked into the dragon's den, head high, heart beating. *She's rich, she's clever, and she's got more clout than you, but she's just another female*, I told myself. I only hoped I could believe it.

ix

Master Merchant Drina Vikk was short and tubby, but her personality seemed to fill the square little room that served as the headquarters for the entire Vikk-shop enterprise. She had a beaky nose set into a round face, a little bow of a mouth that was usually folded into a disapproving pout, and a pair of blue eyes that drilled into me. She wore a rusty-black dress in the frilled and furbel-lowed style of twenty years ago, with a little lace doo-dad covering her graying hair. She sat in an armchair at a small table near the window that looked out on the back garden, where someone was busily weeding veg-etables. No merely pretty flowers for the Vikks—every-thing in the place was meant to be used, and had been well used for a long time, judging by the tears in the carpet and the scratches on the table.

Junior Merchant Betriz and her sister slipped into the room and stood behind their mother, with Baroney next to them, a solid immovable object for me to batter with my irresistible force.

Master Merchant Drina Vikk looked me over. "Who are you, and what do you want with me?"

I gave her my blandest smile. "I am Independent Eye Pola Drach, and I am here at the request of Master As-sassin Fee M'Farr, because he was truly distressed that something had occurred in this house, and he wanted to assure you that it was not something he sanctioned."

"Oh?" Elder Vikk put a world of meaning into that one syllable. "What you mean is, Master Assassin Fee wants to make sure I don't withdraw my support for his Guild."

"I see you don't waste anything, especially not words," I said. "That is quite true. After all, Elder Vikk, why should you continue to pay for a service that has clearly not been provided? If the unfortunate female in question did, in truth, fall down the stairs, then there is nothing more to be said; but if, as the Dark Ones insist, she did not, then the question remains—How did she pass from life, and by whose hand? Master Assassin Fee wants to assure you that whoever did this was in no way connected with his Guild."

"And why would anyone question the demise of that female was an accident?" Drina said, stubbornly clinging to her original statement.

"Well," I said slowly, "for one thing, no one seems to have heard her fall. That's a very long flight of stairs, Elder Vikk. Someone falling down it must have made some noise. According to the Dark One who examined her, she was already gone when he got there. She must have been there for some time. Yet no one roused the house when she fell? Very odd, don't you think?"

"We do not keep late hours in this house," the old female pronounced. "We dine at sundown, and do not waste fuel on artificial light."

That explained Teedo's evening expedition, I thought. Aloud, I said, "Junior Merchant Betriz, did you hear or see anything out of the ordinary that evening?"

The girl glanced at her mother, then squeaked out, "Nothing, Eye Drach. We had dinner, and then I read to Mam, and then we went to bed."

"What about Marla Lily? Did she accompany you up the stairs?" I asked.

"There was no need," Elder Vikk said, scornfully.

"In that case," I pointed out, "how could she have gotten up the stairs in the first place? It appears to me, Elder Vikk, that she was deliberately killed, and by someone in this house." I laid it on thick, watching the old female wince at the vulgarity of my language. Deliberately using terms like *death* and *killing* is just not done, not in Lorr.

"Deliberately?" she echoed. "Why?"

I shrugged apologetically. "For one thing, Elder Vikk, you might not be too pleased at your son's choice of a life-mate."

"Teedo is a fool, easily seduced by a pretty face. The matter could have been resolved in other, less unpleasant ways."

"Are you aware, Elder Vikk, that Merchant Teedo has been seen in some, um, unpleasant places?" I went on. "With some very odd companions. Including, Merchant-Banker Kaisrin, your spouse?"

Kaisrin stiffened at that piece of information. "My spouse's activities are none of your concern, Eye Drach," she said loftily.

"Probably not," I said. "But his name has been linked with Merchant Teedo's in a Post Six notation, and a Clothier's Model was cited as a mutual acquaintance. If you thought that Marla Lily was attempting to separate your spouse from yourself, you would have had a good reason to kill her."

"That is absurd!" Kaisrin snapped. "Devon is not going to separate from me, no matter what evil-minded gossip says."

"Of course not," added Elder Vikk. "He knows where his bread is buttered. Banking is all very well, but the real money is in the shops. Devon Delrey may not be the brightest wick in the chandelier, but he's not about to step away from the Vikk stipend."

"And then there's someone else," I said slowly. "Maybe someone who has the good of the Vikk family at heart, even if he, or she, isn't actually a part of it by blood." I looked at Baroney.

"How's your arm, Servant Baroney? It looks a little stiff. Been walking by the river, lately?"

"What are you saying?" Elder Vikk's eyes narrowed. "Servant Baroney has been with me for years. He was my Dear Olber's companion when they did their Guards service together in the Merchant's War. He would never, ever stoop to anything that would hurt the Vikk family."

"Maybe, maybe not," I said. "But you might think about where he was last night when someone tried to attack me the same way Marla Lily was killed. Meanwhile, accept my condolences on the loss of a prospective relation."

"You may leave!" It was an official order, and it was obeyed. I nodded and stepped aside, so Baroney could let me out of the room. I wasn't going to have that ex-Guard behind me again.

He opened the front door to let me out.

"She would have destroyed the House of Vikk with her mindless extravagance," he said.

"Possibly," I said. "But like Master Merchant Vikk said, there are other ways. She could have been bought off."

"More expense," he grumbled. Then: "What are you going to do?" he asked, a note of fear in his voice.

"I'm going to do what I'm being paid to do," I said. "I'm going to report to Master Assassin Fee M'farr."

And off I went, down Striver's Hill, leaving him open-mouthed behind me.

x

The Master Assassin was right on time.

"What do you have for me?" he demanded.

"Servant Baroney did it,' I said bluntly. "He's an ex-Guardsman, he knows how to kill by hand. He must have come up behind her and done it short and sharp. Then he laid her down at the foot of the stairs and sent for the Dark Ones."

"How do you know?"

"A few things didn't quite add up, even after taking Dark Kelvin's findings into account. No one admits to having heard anyone fall down those stairs. Marla Lily was in evening dress, and had no reason to go up the stairs if the dining room was on the main floor. Nothing you can take to the Guards, though. You can't arrest a man because his hands were wet when he handed the Dark One a basin."

"Wet hands? What's that got to do with anything?" Fee sputtered.

"He'd handled the victim," I reminded him. "Of course he'd wash his hands afterward. And he still smelled of the soap and incense used to purge ill-luck. Oh, yes, Master Assassin, this was definitely a private killing, nothing for the Guild to worry about."

Fee considered what I'd said, then put down another silver.

"That's for handling things quietly," he said, and turned to go.

"Just one more thing." He turned back to me. "You know, Master Assassin, I was wondering just why you picked me for this little job. Like I said yesterday, you've got plenty of investigators in the Guild, and you've probably got a few of the Guards on your payroll as well. So, why me?

"And then it came to me—I'm known for one thing no one else handles. None of the other Eyes will touch Domestics.. So, then I start doing some basic arithmetic. Marla Lily's little package was well on its way before she even met up with Teedo. The only conclusion I could come to is that Marla Lily was one of yours, and so was her offspring-to-be. I'm sorry for your loss, Master Assassin."

Fee's cheeks reddened, then paled. "Marla Lily was more than just 'one of mine'. She was the best, and the brightest, and I really cared for her. We weren't espoused, but I trained her, and she was dear to me."

"She was working Teedo," I guessed. "My guess? Something to do with the funny money that's going around? The Forgers must be having a fit."

"That's Guild business," Master Assassin Fee snapped. "If Marla Lily was killed because of the false coin, the Guild will take care of it. I just wanted to find out whether or not she'd been tapped, that's all. Now I know she wasn't, so it's finished." He slammed the door on his way out.

I sat back in my chair and fingered the coin in front of me, waiting for it to turn. When it didn't, I pocketed it and went to Jake and Holly's. Now I could buy that nice suit, the one that matched my coloring. I felt I'd earned it.

INTERLUDE

YOU'D THINK THAT WOULD BE THE END OF THE MAR-la Lily business, but it wasn't. Not quite. I checked the posts for the next two days, and sure enough, right at the bottom of Post Six, where you'd need to stand on your head or squat into the dust to see it, I found a small notice.

> Drawn from the water: the body of a man in servant's livery, found by the Bargemen's Guild. Identified by Teedo Vikk as Baroney, their Chief Servant, who had just been pensioned off. The death is being described as accidental.

Of course, I said to myself. If you really want the job done right, you call in a professional.

BAD MERCH

I THOUGHT I'D SEEN THE LAST OF THE VIKK CLAN, BUT who should walk into my office three weeks after I finished the job for Fee M'Farr but Kaisrin Vikk, with a simple demand.

"I want you to find out where my spouse gets his money."

Kaisrin, the eldest offspring of the redoubtable Master Merchant Drina Vikk, was a well-dressed, well-bred, well-preserved, and very well-fixed female, thanks to the Vikk-shops that proliferated every district in Lorr. She sat on the uncomfortable wooden chair across from me. I sat in a much more comfortable padded chair behind the desk in my tiny office.

I looked her over while she fidgeted. She'd come to me, she hadn't sent for me to come to her, not usual for the Upper Tier. Of course, the Vikks weren't exactly Upper Tier. They were just rich.

"Your spouse being Devon Delrey." I didn't have to add *of the Banking Delreys*. That went without saying. "I thought the Delrey clan had plenty of coin."

"There have been reverses in the Delrey Banking operations," Kaisrin said. "Devon has his stipend as a Regulator of the Delrey Bank, of course, but he receives another from the Vikk-shops as part of our union settlement. Three weeks ago, he requested an increase, but was refused."

"I suppose there was a reason for the request?"

Kaisrin's lips tightened. "He wanted to purchase an interest in an airship. He explained it quite clearly to me. He and his associates want to use the airship to carry small packages and a few passengers from Lorr to Pangkot and the Southern Territories."

"His associates being your sibling Teedo?"

"And Devon's sibling Selva. Selva explained it to me quite clearly. She is very enthusiastic about the scheme. She thinks it will be quite profitable."

"And Master Merchant Vikk doesn't?"

"It is a very risky venture. Airships are expensive, difficult to control, not easily come by." Kaisrin scowled. "I suggested they consult our sibling Affrey, whose exploits in the Aerial Corps have made him an expert in the field of aeronautics, before they invest in such a scheme. Unfortunately, Affrey is not available for consultation at this time."

In my opinion, airships are best left to the Aerial Corps and the boffins and techs who build and run them. I admit they are useful in keeping an eye on weather conditions, alerting shipping to approaching storms; and if someone from Pangkot decided to try a sea-raid, it would be a good idea to know about it in advance. A few of the

Upper Tier of Admin have them, to carry them to their mountainside retreats, but private airships are enormously expensive, have to be housed in huge barns, need a staff of experts to run them, and, in the long run, aren't worth the coin.

Kaisrin went on. "I thought Devon had given up on the idea, but some days ago, I received a communication from a person claiming to be the owner of a privately-built airship requesting verification of a deposit into my personal account of some twenty thousand in silver. I had not deposited such funds, but there they were."

"And you think Devon has been using your personal account to squirrel away funds for this scheme?"

"I don't know what to think. I cannot let him think I don't trust him, but I know I never deposited anything like that sum, and I would never use it for such a wild venture as setting up an airship freight and passenger line."

"So," I said, reaching into the desk drawer for my standard form. "What, exactly, do you want me to do?"

"I want you to find out where the money came from," Kaisrin repeated.

"And when I do?"

"Tell me, and I will take what action I deem necessary." She reached for the purse that hung from her belt. "I believe your rate is one silver a day."

"That's the going rate," I said. It buys a day of lurking—spying, if you like. I call it Eyeing. I reminded the client of one more thing. "You realize I'm supposed to report any illegal activity I discover to Administration."

"You think my husband is involved in something illegal?" Kaisrin's voice rose.

"I think *you* do," I countered. "Otherwise, why come to me? The Merchants' Guild has plenty of spies of their own. Master Merchant Drina Vikk is a major contributor to the Merchants' Guild treasury. You could find one of their people easy enough. I'm an Independent. No Guild, no badge, no sigil."

Kaisrin's face relaxed into a wry grin. "No alliances, either, Eye Drach. You are not beholden to anyone, least of all my mother. Anything I say or do at the Merchants' Guild-Hall will get back to her, and I would prefer that she did not know Devon is spending money he does not have or putting illicit funds into my personal account."

That made sense. Master Merchant Drina Vikk was a staunch Conservationist, one of the group who are convinced that all of Lorr's resources are finite, therefore, don't waste any of them. It's a good excuse to be thrifty to the point of miserliness; but in Lorr, you're allowed to go your own way, as long as it doesn't involve pain to anyone or anything else .

"Besides…" Kaisrin's expression hardened. "You were involved in a previous incident regarding our family. I do not have to explain myself further." She got up from the hard wooden chair and laid out three silvers. "This will pay for your first three days. If it takes longer than that, I will continue to pay until you report to me."

"You'll meet me here?" I shoved the form at her, with the stylus and inkwell, so she could sign off on the deal.

"No," she said. She gave it some thought, then said, "Vikk Franchises maintains an office in the Merchants' Guild Hall. You may send your report there. Mark it confidential to me."

"I prefer to report in person," I said. "Some things shouldn't be written down."

"In that case," Kaisrin said, "you may find me at my mother's house on Striver's Hill most mornings. My afternoons are otherwise occupied."

And that was that. She turned on her well-shod heel and hustled out, through the alley to the space in front of Jake and Holly's where she had left her pedishaw and driver.

I was ready to start out when I heard a timid tap on the door, and another female edged her way in. This one was small, brown, slender, wrapped in a length of cotton that wound around her to make a skirt, with another end over her head. *Desert refugee*, I thought, and sank back into my chair.

She looked me over, then said, "You are Pola Drach?"

I admitted that I was. She looked doubtful. Maybe she expected someone large and fierce, like Basher Bob, or an overweight eccentric, like The Brain. I'm medium-sized, with washed-out blond hair, honey-gold skin, green eyes, not well-dressed. An Independent Eye has to fade into the background, and I do that very well.

"The person at the Guard-House said you can help me," she said. "My husband is missing."

"And you want me to find him," I finished for her. "Why not the City Guards?"

"Because he is not important," the woman said."I am Drushka, only a franchise shopkeeper and not a true merchant. Yonah and me, we come here from Pangkot to be together. His family and mine, they would not let us marry. He is a Scribe, I am only a Desert person, bound to service in his house. We love each other, we want to be together. Yonah said we will run to Lorr, where we can be together."

It sounded like a sappy mag story—warring families, youthful lovers. I waited for her to finish.

"Yonah could not find work as a Scribe here—he was not qualified, and when we tried to sell things in the market—my bracelets and rings—to get us money to live on, we were taken into the Merchants' Guild-Hall and told that we must pay more and more, just to sell things. Then came someone and said that if we wished to do so, we could become Franchisees, under the umbrella of Master Merchant Drina Vikk."

I had a good idea where this was going, but I gave her time to collect her thoughts.

Drushka took another breath, and went on with her tale.

"It was a good deal, said this person. If we paid a sum, we would be given a shop to run. We would pay for the stock, but less than if we tried to get it for ourselves, and we would pay a portion of the rental of the shop, and we could charge what we liked for the stock, once it was paid for, and keep the profit for ourselves. There was a lodging-place behind the shop where Yonah and I could stay, and a food-market nearby, and it seemed to be the best thing to do, so we did it."

And that's how you get sucked in, I thought. Of course, the payments on the stock and the rental of the shop were never quite covered by the profits, so the Franchisees got into debt. And in Lorr, you have to pay off your debts before you can leave. Some Vikk Franchisees did well enough, some didn't; it depended how well-off the neighborhood was, and how well they managed their money.

"How well did it work out for you?" I asked, taking in her cheap cotton wrapper and scuffed sandals.

"Very well, at first," she said. "In a year, we paid off our initial debt, and were able to find a larger set of rooms, and a little garden–plot, where I could raise a few vegetables, which we could sell, besides the stock we got from Merchant Vikk. And we were able to be Merchants' Guild members, although we were not full voters, because of being Franchisees, but we could allow Merchant Vikk to speak for us at the Merchant's Council meetings. It was good, for a while.

"But it has not been good, not at all, not recently." She started to weep. I reached into the drawer and handed her one of the cotton nose-wipes I keep there (bought, I must say, at my local Vikk-shop).

"Sales bad?" I asked sympathetically.

"We were given stock that no one would buy," Drushka said, suddenly fierce. "It was bad merchandise. I knew it was bad."

"Rotten stuff?" This would really put the Vikk franchise out of business in a hurry. The Merchants' Guild comes down very hard on anyone who tries to foist bad merch onto the public.

"Not rotten, not spoiled, just not good," Drushka said. "We sell many things—small things for the house, pots, pans, soaps and facepaints, even books sometimes. We also sell clet, ground and packaged, for easy cooking."

Clet. It would be. I loathe the stuff. I don't care if it's touted by the boffins as being totally local, not brought by the Founders. They can yammer all they like about how healthful it is, how much the alkaloid in it does for the heart and liver. To me it smells like wet socks, and tastes worse.

But everyone else in Lorr loves it, and you can't get two feet in any street without coming across a stand or a shop where it's being offered, hot or cold, boiled or brewed, with or without sweetener. My morning pick-me-up is chai, but like the slogan says, "Everything in Lorr runs on clet".

"And this shipment was spoiled?" I prompted her.

"It was not spoiled. It was not rotten. It is just…wrong. There is clet that comes already ground—you put it into a special pot with a sieve and run the hot water through the roasted beans—but this is a powder. You are supposed to put it into the hot water in a cup, and it will come into clet, but it tastes bad—weak and nasty. Our people would not buy it, and we could not sell it, but we had it.

"And then the people who used to come to our shop went to another one, in the next street, because they said that if we sold bad clet, we would sell other bad things. And Yonah told the man who came for our payment that he would not take any more of this clet, and he would go to the Merchants' Guild and complain that we were not getting our proper stock, and we would not sell bad merchandise, it was wrong, and the Gods would punish us."

Drushka stopped to wipe her eyes and nose, and I had a very nasty picture in my mind. I could see where this was going, and I didn't like it, not one bit.

"Yonah went out three days ago to the Merchants' Guild, to tell them what he told that man," Drushka said.

"And he didn't come back," I said. It wasn't a question.

Drushka nodded. "So, I went to the Guard-House, like I said, but the Guard laughed at me and said that Yonah was probably off with the Licensees, and I should wait until he came home. But the other Guard, a female one, said I should go to Clothiers' Alley and ask for Pola Drach, that Drach was an Independent Eye and would help me."

I made a mental note to find out which of the City Guards this was. I don't get all that many recommendations from the Guards, and I owed a debt to this one.

"What do you want me to do?" I asked.

"Find out what happened to Yonah," Drushka said fiercely.

"If I find out something…unfortunate…happened?"

I didn't want to put it too bluntly. No one in Lorr utters the word *death*. It's just not done. It's been that way ever since the Founders landed, all those generations ago.

"Then I will know, and I will do what has to be done," Drushka said. Her mouth firmed up, and she stopped cry-ing. "It is the waiting that is so bad." She fumbled under the wrapper for her purse. "I do not know your fee, but I have some money left from my dowry…"

"Give me three bits," I said. "That will pay me for three days."

"That is not much," Drushka said. "I do not wish to be indebted to you."

"I have a sliding scale," I assured her. "Besides, I don't like bad merch, and I really don't like the kind of people who'd hand lousy clet off to the public, even if I don't much care for the stuff myself."

Drushka made a sign over my face that was some kind of Desert Folk blessing. I handed her the form. She looked at it and the stylus.

"I do not have the letters," she said simply.

I read the form out to her, wrote her name, and told her, "Make a mark here. It'll serve."

She took the stylus in hand and put down a squiggle that might have been anything. If what I thought had happened happened, I'd have a sad chore ahead of me.

"I'll need a picture of him," I said.

"I have this." She reached under the wrapper and took out a little drawing showing her with a scrawny little specimen with round lenses in front of his eyes. "This we got when we were first here. To mark our union," she added.

Espousal picture, of course, with him looking proudly ahead and her looking fondly at him. Nothing special about him, except the lenses; you could see a dozen of him in any of the offices in any of the Guild Halls in Lorr. Of course, being from Pangkot, he wouldn't have the

Lorr letters, or the connections for the Guild Halls, so he was happy enough with his Vikk-shop. There were hundreds like him on the back streets of Lorr, in the Fishmarket and Industrial sectors and across the river in Flatlands, doing their daily chores, raising families, growing small plots of vegetables, keeping Lorr thriving.

"You will find him," she said.

"One way or another," I said. "You can come back here in three days, and I will tell you what I have found out."

"No," she said, "I cannot leave the shop. Today, I asked my neighbor to mind it, but I must get back before her children come home from their lessons. You can come to me—the Vikk-shop two streets off the Main Road in Fishmarket Sector, next to the food-stall that makes kebabs." She made the Blessing sign again, and left me thinking over what had been said, and what hadn't been said, by two women, both worried about their men.

I had three silvers and three bits. Now I had to earn them.

ii

Where to begin? With the obvious—go to the biggest gossips in Lorr and then check the News Posts.

Jake and Holly are the top-of-the-line clothiers in Lorr, always ahead of the market with the finest fabrics, the most original designs. They were not happy when I showed up in their showroom.

"Are you trying to put us out of business?" Holly yelled at me before I even closed the door behind me.

"Letting Merchant Kaisrin Vikk park her pedishaw here!" Jake exploded behind her.

"What's wrong with that?" I looked from round, red-haired Holly to long, fair-haired Jake.

"She's a dowd!" Holly told me. "She wears the same things, year in, year out, hasn't changed her style since never!"

"Classic," I said. I headed for the changing booths, and a special cabinet where I kept a few odds and ends.

"Dowdy," Jake repeated firmly.

"People who buy from us want the latest, not the last," Holly said.

"All we need is for word to get out on Post Six that Kaisrin Vikk was seen coming out of our establishment, and we're ruined with the up-and-comers," Jake moaned. "The Admin debs won't touch us if they think we sell to the old Striver's Hill crowd."

"Why not make dowdy the new chic?" I said.

Holly made a face at me. "Not funny, Drach. And what if someone starts the rumor we're peddling knock-offs to the Vikk-shops?"

"Then you'll have another source of income," I said.

"We will not!" Jake looked down his nose at me, which is quite a feat, since he has a lot of nose to look down. "We do not sell knock-offs. Our designs are exclusives, and we do not reproduce them for anyone, let alone the sort of clientele that frequent Vikk-shops."

"Our people won't buy from us if they think every little office drone is going to have the same thing tomorrow," Holly stated. "And if the mechs and techs start wearing them, we'd be ruined for sure."

They followed me into the fitting-rooms. I ducked into the last try-on booth at the end of the row and opened the wall panel hiding my private cabinet. I fished out a particular blue cotton jacket to wear over my slightly shabby white shirt, and put a colorful silk scarf in one of the pockets. Now I looked like every little office drone, which was exactly the effect I wanted. I twisted my not-quite-blond hair into a knot on my neck, with a few strands loose to make me look frazzled. I checked the result in the try-on mirror. No one would remember what I looked like as soon as I passed by, and that was perfect.

Jake and Holly were still yammering when I emerged from the booth.

"All right, all right!" I held up a hand for silence. "Look, if someone puts something on Post Six, you can always claim that Kaisrin Vikk has decided to change her style and came to Jake and Holly's because you're exactly what she isn't. Either that, or you can start a new line, call it Classic, and make it work. If you make it, she'll buy it, and wear it."

"And we'll get known as the Dowdy House," Holly moaned.

"Then charge her triple," I said.

"We should raise your rent," Jake groused.

I ignored that one. They owed me more than I did them, and they knew it.

I sauntered over to the News Posts at the end of Clothier's Alley where it opens onto Market Street. Post One was all about the latest raids on shipping and hints the military wasn't cracking down on the sea raiders hard enough, with more hints that the Autocrat of Pangkot might know more about said raids than he let on. Post Two had the latest Council news, and a strong message from the Craftsmen's Guild regarding the Merchants' Guild's latest statement regarding raising the percentage on product.

Post Three had the largest crowd, checking the latest financial listings. Post Four was covered with notices of concerts, plays, and other entertainment. Post Five had another large crowd, arguing over the latest basher-bout results.

My goal was Post Six, where the anonymous gossip was stuck. I checked the ones at the very top, then the bottom of the column where the obituaries are placed. Sure enough, all the way at the very bottom was a tiny slip of paper with the City Guards seal on it. The body of a male had been found in the Warehouse District—no sigil, no badge, anyone who could identify him should apply to the Dark Ones.

Drushka wouldn't have seen this notice, even if she could read Lorran, not unless she was looking for it.

A pattern was forming in my mind. Not a good one, either. I wasn't sure where Devon Delrey's mysterious good fortune fit in, but I somehow thought it did.

The next piece of the puzzle was right in front of me, across the Central Plaza at the Merchants' Guild Hall. I headed towards it, plotting the next moves in this game.

iii

The Merchants' Guild Hall dominates the Central Plaza of Lorr. It's big and shiny, four stories high, capped with

53

a dome covered with chips of mica that shimmer in the sunlight; and like the Merchant Founders, it's out to impress anyone and everyone with the vital importance of Trade in Lorr. It's full of busy people, or people trying to look busy. Mostly office drones in gray or blue trou or skirts and jackets, following their bosses, the Master Merchants, most of whom maintained a presence in the Guild Hall even though their main offices were in the brick hives behind the plaza.

I got in easily enough. Once inside, I turned the blue cotton jacket inside-out to reveal a faded lining in a swirly pattern typical of the Desert folk. I wound the scarf around my hair and covered half my face. Nothing I could do about green eyes, but I hoped no one would look hard enough to notice them.

I dove back into the crowd, acting the part of a frightened Desert refugee while I looked helplessly about me. Finally, one of the Merchants' functionaries asked what I wanted.

"I am looking for where I can sell things," I said in my most unintelligible Desert accent. "I am told to come here. I wish to sell things," I repeated, as if I had memorized the words. "I am told there is a place where I will be given things to sell."

The functionary, a stout woman in a prim trou-and-shirt set, smiled briefly. "I suppose you want to work with the Vikk franchise," she said.

"Yes, yes," I said, nodding eagerly. "That is the name I am told will let me sell things."

The woman made a face and pointed me towards one of the many hallways leading out of the central lobby.

"Up those stairs, to the right. This way!"

I started off in the wrong direction, and she put out a hand to turn me around, then thought better of it and yelled instead.

I trotted off, and sure enough, there was an office with the Vikk sigil—interlocked D and O initials—on the door. Inside was a waiting-room, where three males and two females sat on benches, and a snappy-looking young sport was stationed behind a desk.

All of them looked up as I edged into the office.

"This is place for selling things?" I asked, sounding like a bad comic actor's version of a Desert refugee.

The sport smiled broadly at me. I could see the wheels turning in his mind—Another sucker!

He didn't say that, however. He greeted me as if I were the one person he'd been trying to find all day.

"Welcome, Friend, to the Vikk-shop Franchise office. We are here to help you."

"I wish to sell things," I said. "How will you help me sell things?"

"We will provide you with things to sell," he said. "Master Merchant Vikk will cover your Merchants' Guild fees, which will allow you to sell merchandise in Lorr under the Regulations, and will find you a location from which to sell said merchandise. You will pay a sum to us to cover the rental of this location, and we will stock it with our own merchandise."

"You give me goods?" I said, pretending to think this over.

"We do not *give* you merchandise," the sport said. "You buy it from us with the profits from what you have already sold once you have covered the initial expense."

"But I make things," I said. "I make pretty things from shells, from beads. I wish to sell them."

I could see the eagerness draining out of him. "If you want to make things, you must go to the Craftsmen's Guild," he explained. "They will direct you to the appropriate Merchant, who will sell them for you."

"But at home, I make things, then I sell them. I keep coins for me," I said stubbornly.

The sport didn't have time for this. "In Lorr, there are Craftsmen, and there are Merchants," he said. "If you make things, you are a Craftsman. If you sell them, you are a Merchant. If you wish to join the Vikk-shop Franchise, you will become a Merchant. You will buy your first shipment of stock, you will pay the rent on the shop, and the rest will be up to you. You may add certain items to the stock, such as fresh produce, but you must use what is provided by Merchant Vikk."

"I think about it," I said, edging out the door.

And I did, while I turned myself back into a Lorran. The scarf went around my neck, the jacket went back to plain blue, and I twitched the skirt a little higher to show some leg. Then I headed for the Complaints Department to see if Franchisee Yonah had ever had a hearing.

The Complaints Department wasn't easy to find— the Merchants' Guild didn't want to admit that anyone ever complained about how they were being treated at any establishment in Lorr. I worked my way around the offices and corridors, up and down a few staircases, and found it at the very top of the building.

Complaints was run by a well-stuffed shirt—male, red-faced, with a fringe of reddish hair and a large red nose—aided by an aged female dragon who kept the books for him. Both of them regarded me as an unwelcome intrusion into their game of cards.

"How's business?" I said politely.

"What do you want?" the female asked, not bothering with the standard response.

"I'd like some information about a complaint," I said, still polite.

"We do not give out such information," the male stated.

"Mostly, I wanted to know if a complaint was lodged," I said. "I'm looking for a Vikk-shop Franchisee named Yonah. According to his wife, he was last seen heading for this department to lodge a complaint."

The two Complaint Managers exchanged a glance, then the female said, "We did not receive a complaint from anyone called Yonah."

"Then Yonah never got here?"

"We have no such person in our records," the male said. He didn't even try to check the files behind him. I should have known better than to ask one of the office drones for anything, but I persisted.

"Do you remember *anyone* making a complaint about the merchandise being offered at the Vikk-shops?" I persisted. "Especially bad clet?"

"None of the clet offered at the Vikkshops is good," sniffed the female.

"But we have had no particular complaints," the male repeated.

"But if you had?"

"Then we would have brought it to the attention of Merchandise Security," the male assured me.

"But no one has complained."

"Not to us," the female said, picking up her cards.

"But to someone?" I muttered, and I left them to it.

So, to Merchandise Security I went. This meant more up-and-down corridors, but I found it at the other end of the Guild Hall, on the ground floor, nowhere near Complaints. The functionaries here were both male, both ex-Guardsmen by the look of them. One of them seemed familiar; I recalled seeing him around the markets, checking on the merch. A tall, skinny type with a long nose, sniffing out spoiled produce and stale baked goods, handing out summonses.

"Oyo, Guardsman Falloon," I greeted him. "How's business?"

"Oyo, Eye Drach," he replied. "Business is good. What brings you to Merchants' Guild Hall? Someone hire you to find a bad fish?"

No point is being coy about it, I thought.

"More like bad clet," I said. "There's a Vikk-shop Franchisee missing. His wife says he was on his way here to lodge a grievance about having to stock bad clet. Complaints says he never did, but that's to be expected. Did he get to you?"

Falloon scratched his long nose and frowned. "Can't say as anyone came in here with a grievance about clet," he said after a while.

"But we'd love to slam the old woman with a hefty fine," the other Guild Security added. This one was shorter, broader, and younger than Falloon. Probably just out of the Guards, or maybe ex-Aerial Corps, which explained his hard language.

"For selling cheap merch?" I asked with a grin. Merchants' Guild has to accept Master Merchant Drina Vikk, and her Franchise, but they don't have to like it.

"For calling those Franchisees 'employees' so they don't pay Guild fees," Falloon said bitterly.

"And we still have to check their stock, to make sure it's legit," the other one said.

"You mean it's not?" I grinned nastily.

"You said it, I didn't," Falloon said. "The Vikks buy up factory lots from who knows where, ship them in on small boats, stock their shops with them, and undercut everyone else."

The other Security type said, "If you know something about bad merch, we'd be very grateful if you let us in on it. It would give us something to go on, some way to put that old biddy out of business." At least he'd modified his language.

"What about the poor folks who put their lives into running the shops?" I said. "They'd be out of business, too."

"Too bad for them," Falloon said with a shrug.

I got back to what had brought me there. "Ever see this character before?"

I took out the wedding picture. Falloon and his pal gave it a look, then Falloon shrugged again.

"Maybe I saw him around Fishmarket Square. There are a lot of Desert folk there, so it would make sense for him to run the Vikk-shop in that district. But I haven't seen him in here, Drach."

I took them at their word. There was no reason for them to lie to me. Franchisee Yonah may have been on his way to the Merchants' Guild hall, but it looked as if he never got there.

There was only one more place he could be, and I didn't really like the idea, but I had to check.

I headed out towards the edge of Lorr, to the Temple of the Dark Ones, with the nasty feeling that Trader Yonah had met with a very bad end.

iv

The one subject no one wants to speak of in Lorr is death. That's what the Dark Ones are for—they handle anything that once lived but does not anymore, whether human or animal. They handle the vermin that get drowned in the gutters, and they are the ones who take bodies for burial. No one wants to keep lifeless things inside Lorr unless they're edible and, even then, only as long as need be. They are dealt with on the outskirts of the city, so the Dead are well away from the Living.

This meant a long trip for me in a carrier, and then a long walk to the Death House, where I would wait some more to speak with a Dark One about the unknown male found on the Waterfront. According to the Post Six notice, it would be held until identified. I told the gatekeeper I could identify it and was there to claim the reward.

Thus, I got into the Dark Ones' temple and was shown into an unadorned room where I'd been a time or two. Dark Kelvin came along, tall and stringy with lank hair flying around his face. His manners hadn't improved since the last time I'd been there, but he wasn't quite so sniffy this time around.

He came right to the point. No niceties, no "How's business?".

"What do you want this time, Eye Drach?"

"I saw a notice that a male body was brought here two nights ago," I said bluntly. "I think it's someone I'm looking for." I showed him the portrait. "Is this the one?"

He frowned at it and gave a very brief nod. "That resembles the one brought in," he admitted. "Do you know the name?"

"He was called Yonah, and he was a Vikk-shop Franchisee," I said. "Can you tell me how he met his end?"

"His body bears the marks of a beating," Kelvin said. "His skull is fractured. His hands were crushed. His ribs are broken, and a lung was punctured. In my opinion, he died of internal bleeding due to the wounds incurred by the beating." He recited it with as much feeling as a shopping list.

"Nasty way to go," I said.

"I suspect he was still alive after the beating was administered," Kelvin said. "His hands show abrasions, as if he had dragged himself along."

"Where was he found, exactly?"

"You would have to request that information of the Guards on duty at the Waterfront," Kelvin said. "They brought him here instead of sending for one of us to see him before he was moved."

That was definitely odd. Most of the City Guards won't have anything to do with the dead. Procedure states that any Guard who discovers a corpse must send for the Dark Ones immediately. No one is to move the body before they examine it. For a Guard to take that kind of action sent a signal to me that something definitely fishy was going on.

Dark Kelvin wasn't happy about it, either. "The whole scene has been contaminated," he declared. "We will never really know, beyond a doubt, what happened to him."

I had a good idea already. I just needed to get the specifics.

Dark Kelvin frowned at me. "You say his name was Yonah? What do you know about him?"

"Only what I was told," I explained. "He's from Pangkot, came here a little over a year ago. From what his spouse told me, I suspect they ran afoul of some of those family restrictions the Desert Folk have. She came to me when he didn't return home a few nights ago. She doesn't read the Posts—she doesn't know Lorr letters."

"Or any others, I suppose," sniffed Dark Kelvin. "Well, Eye Drach, it will be your sad duty to inform her that her spouse is here. She may make whatever arrangements she likes at the City Temple." He turned to go, then turned back and looked me over with a speculative gleam in his eye. "Eye Drach," he said. "You came to my notice in the matter of Marla Lily. I admire your persistence in uncovering the one responsible for her death. It betokens intelligence on your part."

"That's very, um, nice for you to say," I said.

"Also, you appear to be in good health," he went on.

"I'm fit for action," I admitted. I still didn't quite know where this was going.

"And your physical appearance is appealing," he added.

I definitely didn't know what to say to that, but I now had an inkling what was going on.

Dark Kelvin cleared his throat. "Ahem! May I ask a personal question?"

"Why not?"

"Are you averse to union with the male sex?"

"Not particularly."

"Are you currently involved with anyone?'

"Not at this time, no."

"Then you will not be offended if I ask whether you will consent to physical intimacy with me," he blurted.

"What!"

"It has been brought to my attention that I have neglected my duty. I have never had offspring, although it is incumbent on all of our Order that we do so." Kelvin's pale face flushed pink.

I tried hard to keep my face straight. Of all the propositions I'd ever had, this was by far the weirdest.

"Dark Kelvin," I said carefully. "I am very flattered you should ask me, but I must decline."

"Is it my appearance that is repugnant?" he asked. "I am not, perhaps, the most attractive of males—"

"It's not that," I said hastily. I didn't want to get on the wrong side of Kelvin—I might need him again. "It's just that…well, if I was to go through all the pain and mess of having a baby, I'd want to keep it by me, and not have it taken away to the Dark Ones' nursery."

Kelvin thought this over. "Perhaps your objection is valid," he said. "I shall consider it. If you ever change your mind, please let me know."

And off he went, hair and robe flapping, leaving me to make my way back to downtown Lorr with a lot to think about.

v

So, now I knew where Franchisee Yonah was, and what had got him there, but was that the whole story? How much did I really owe Drushka?

I suppose most people would say my job was done. All I had to do was go to Drushka and tell her that her spouse was in the Dark Ones' temple. After all, she'd only paid three bits, not even enough for a bag of potting soil for Ficus.

Still, something was nagging at me. How did a small shopkeeper rate that kind of a beating over clet?

I headed for the next stop—the City Guard House. Good citizenship required that I identify the body. Good Eyeing required that I find out more about how he got to the Dark Ones' temple.

I didn't see anyone I knew at the Guard House. It was late in the afternoon, change of shift. The character behind the desk was a hardbitten old sod who looked like she'd seen everything and hated all of it.

"Guard Wanda," I said, reading her name off her badge. "I am Independent Eye Pola Drach, come to report on the unidentified male found beaten to death two nights ago."

64

"I've heard about you, Drach," she said, not even giving me the courtesy of a title. "What's this fellow to you?"

"His spouse was worried when he didn't come home two nights ago. She hired me to find out where he was. I'm going to have to tell her he's been picked up and put in the Dark One's temple."

"You're sure of this?" Guard Wanda snapped.

"I got identification corroboration from Dark Kelvin himself," I said. "He also told me the body'd been moved before the Dark Ones could examine the scene. That's against procedure, isn't it?"

Guard Wanda gave me the hard-eye. "Procedure being something you know about, eh?"

I tried another approach. "Look, Guard Wanda, I've got to go tell Franchisee Drushka that her spouse is not coming home. She's going to want to know how, and why."

"Not my business."

"At least tell me where the body was found," I said.

Guard Wanda made an exasperated noise. "Then go to the Waterfront District Guardhouse and ask *them*." *And see if that does any good*, she didn't say but I knew she meant.

Another carrier ride over to the Waterfront and the Guardhouse near the bridge, where I recognized at least two of the Guards, mostly because they hung out at Smokey Joe's. Guard Tommas had been in my unit when I'd seen something I shouldn't have and reported it to my superiors. He'd seen the same indiscretion, but he hadn't reported it. Instead, he'd kept it to himself, more or less.

Now he was stationed at the Waterfront, and I was Independent, which shows how things work in Lorr.

"Oyo, Drach," he greeted me. "How's business? What brings you to the Waterfront?"

"Oyo, Tommas. Business is good. I'm Eyeing for the spouse of the male you found two days ago."

He made a sympathetic noise. "Real shame, that. Poor fella must have run into some hardbodies and made a stink. Happens a lot. Fella wants a good time, can't afford to pay, gets it taken out of his hide."

"Only, I don't think he was down here for a good time," I said. "His spouse says not."

"They always do," Guard Tommas said with a wink.

"Where did you find him?" I asked.

"We didn't," Tommas said. "He was dumped on our doorstep."

"Or maybe dragged himself?" I said. "The Dark One who examined him said there were abrasions on his hands."

"He might have," Tommas admitted. "But he was gone before we could do anything to help. We shipped him over to the Dark Ones before he could stink the place up and posted the notice."

"I've been to the Dark Ones, and I've been to the Guard House," I said virtuously. "His name, for your records, is Yonah; he was a Vikk-shop Franchisee."

Tommas nodded wisely. "Like I figured. Shopkeeper out for a night's drinking, got to the wrong place. It's a shame for the spouse, but it happens on the Waterfront." He got out the ledger and ran a finger down the list of incidents. "At least now we can adjust the record book. Thank you, Eye Drach, for your information."

"I wish I could say the same," I said. "But I've got a lot more questions than answers. How did Franchisee Yonah get here in the first place? Who beat him up, and why?"

"That's your job, isn't? Asking questions?" Guard Tommas sneered. "Good luck with that on the Waterfront. Ask the wrong question, you just might wind up like Yonah."

"I'll bear that in mind," I said, and off I went into the gathering dusk for the one chore I'd been dreading. I didn't want to drag this out any longer. I'd have to tell Drushka she was alone in Lorr, because Yonah wasn't ever coming home again.

vi

Fishmarket Sector isn't far from the Waterfront. The fishing boats tie up at the piers; the fish get hauled off and sold to the fishmongers, who haul them two streets away to the Fishmarket. There, the good householders of Lorr can pick up their dinners and be sure they are fresh. Fish are plentiful in the river and across the estuary, and at least you know what you've got when you eat a fish. Roast beast isn't always identifiable. It could be mammal or fowl or reptile, and sometimes it's hard to tell one from the other after it's been chopped, stewed, or doused with veg-sauce.

By now, it was almost dark, and most of the shops had closed for the night. The fishstalls were empty except for the feral felines who prowled around looking for scraps and fighting over fishheads and tails. A breeze had picked up over the river, disbursing some of the heat that had banked in the close quarters of the oldest part of Lorr, originally built for mechs and techs from the Founders' Ships. Most of them had moved to Industrial Sector or across the river to Flatlands, leaving the old prefabs for refugees and other lowlifes to take over.

I scouted around for Drushka's shop. There were at least three other Vikk-shops on the streets leading off the Fishmarket, and it took a while before I found the right one.

There was no mistaking it, once I got there. A squad of bearded, long-shirted, baggy-pantsed Desert males were outside, a rank of pedishaws lined up in the street. That made sense—a lot of the recent refugees had nothing to offer but strong legs and hard backs, and the Transport Guild was willing to offer employment for public pedishaw drivers.

I stepped up to the door of the shop. One of the Desert males stood in my way. I looked him straight in the eye, an affront to his Desert male dignity, and announced myself.

"I am Independent Eye Drach, here to report to Franchisee Drushka. Let me pass!"

"You are not wanted here!" he said curtly.

"Friend Driver" I said with a false smile, "I have been hired to do work for Franchisee Drushka. I am here because I have to complete that task. Now, are you going to keep me from doing what I have been paid to do, or are you going to let me in?"

He sneered, "You are a woman!"

I took a deep breath and let it out again. "Friend Driver, you have probably not been here in Lorr long enough to know of our history. Therefore, I will inform you of something every child in Lorr learns as soon as they know their letters.

"When the Founders came here, they decided that if a task had to be done, it would be done, no matter by whom, and that gender did not apply. Therefore, Friend Driver, it is considered very impolite to remark on the gender of persons in Lorr, particularly to use the terms 'woman' or 'man'.

"I tell you this because someday you may encounter a female in authority who has less patience with Desert nonsense than I do, and she will clap you into the Guardhouse for insolence! Now, Friend Driver, will you let me in, or do I have to resort to violence?"

I opened my coat to show my small bludgeon.

The big Desert character moved aside, and I went through the shop to the living quarters beyond the showroom, where a squad of Desert females surrounded Drushka, all veils and filmy skirts and bangles and beads.

Drushka let out long howl when she saw my face.

"He is dead!" she shrieked. "I could sense it! He is gone to Paradise!"

The rest of the pack howled something in the Desert tongue and started to chant.

I bowed awkwardly. I hate this part of the job, but I do it because the client deserves to have someone tell them bad news in person.

"I have found your husband," I told Drushka. "He is at the Dark Ones' temple, on the outskirts of Lorr."

"How…?"

"He was beaten," I said, aware of the females around me, and the males clustered by the door unwilling to intrude on the female quarters but curious to find out what had happened to their friend. "I don't know who did it.

I can find out, if you want me to go ahead. All you asked me to do was find him, and I've done that. The rest is up to you. I can continue to ask questions until I get an answer that satisfies me. Or, I can stop and let you grieve."

Drushka nodded fiercely. "You are not finished," she said. "I paid you for three days. You have barely given me one day."

"I can return your money," I said.

Drushka didn't even hesitate. "Continue, Eye Drach. Find out who did this thing."

"And then what?" I asked, although I had a pretty good idea.

"I will have justice," Drushka said, and stared at the Desert males in the doorway.

"Have you eaten?" That was a stout Desert female, holding a platter of dried fruits under my nose.

"Not yet," I admitted. I was hungry, but Desert food and clet aren't my kind of supper. Still, it wouldn't do for me to refuse the hospitality, considering I'd already insulted a male.

"You must eat," Drushka insisted. "And drink clet. Not the bad stuff, the good clet. We make it in the proper fashion."

I had to sit on a pile of cushions and sip from a tiny cup of the stuff, sweetened with honey to the point of nausea. The Desert food was loaded with spices that burned my tongue, and by the time I left, I was ready to head for home and my own bottle of cool chai and mint.

My digs were undisturbed, which was refreshing. I swilled down a measure of chai, picked at some leftover fowl from last night's meal, and gave Ficus a good squirt of the chai. Ficus perks up when it's given a nice spritz.

"I don't like this at all," I told Ficus while I ate. "There's a racket going down, that's for sure, but the question is, is it someone at the Fatsos playing games, or is it someone setting up for themselves? Either way, I may be stirring up a hornets' nest. Let's hope I don't get stung too badly."

I spent the rest of the evening sauntering up and down Entertainment Row picking up news and gossip, mostly about the new ships coming into the Waterfront and the Pangkoti sailors on them, who were being rowdy in the lower-class taverns. There were some choice words about Captain Ishka Kunine's recent liaison with Selva Delrey, and some more about Teedo Vikk and his choice of play-mates; but nothing about Vikk-shops or bad clet. I retired to my digs, trying to make sense of things. There must be a pattern; I just couldn't see it.

vii

Next morning, I did the usual, took care of Ficus, and dressed in a nondescript walking-around outfit—black trou, gray shirt, blue-gray jacket with a modest design of silver braid on the sleeves and hem. Hair tucked un-der a scarf that could be tied up on the head or under the chin. Most important, stout walking-shoes and a net-bag carryall—I was going to do a lot of walking and wanted my feet to be up to it, and I expected to do some shopping while I was at it.

I spent the morning meandering the back streets of Lorr—Fishmarket near the river, Industrial a bit more inland, Gardener's at the base of the encircling hills that made the Founders settle here in the first place. I wandered through the Market District, where the Merchants have their main offices, and the Shopping Sector between Central Plaza and Grand Boulevard. I covered most of the space between the river and the hills.

In other words, I went clear through all of Lorr, and there were Vikk-shops in almost every sector, every block or so, with the possible exception of Arriver's Hill, Strivers' Hill, and the Grand Boulevard, where the most exclusive shops and the most luxurious of the Licensed houses were.

I went in and out of various Vikk-shops, chatted with the Franchisees, picked up all sorts of goods, and noticed a few things.

For one, a lot of the Franchisees were some kind of newcomer to Lorr. Westerners down from the mountains, Desert Folk fleeing the drought, Southern refugees from the strife in Pangkot. All of them seeking a better life in Lorr, where there were no restrictions on how you live or what you think, only who can or can't do business through one or the other of the Guilds.

In each of the shops, I double-checked the clet. There was a definite difference in the stock. Some was in glass jars with a green label, some with a blue label. The Franchisees with the blue-label clet were in the poorest districts, and almost all of them had that look in their eyes that told me they were under pressure to sell the stuff fast.

I glanced into the storerooms in the back as I wandered in and out of shops. Barrels of pickled fish, crates of jars, all with the sigil of the Dockers' Guild that showed they'd been properly offloaded and marked. But there were some crates that didn't have that sigil. I brushed against one, and it clinked. Glass jars inside? Suspect clet? Not offloaded by the proper Guild, and not marked for tax purposes? I started to get a picture of what was going down.

I felt the eyes on my back as I left the last of the Vikk-shops in Industrial Sector.. I glanced into the nearest shop window and saw a hardbody—couldn't miss that swagger—taller than most, with a scar across his neck where someone had tried to carve his head from his shoulders, a heavy bludgeon swinging from his belt. He wore black leather decorated with silver studs to emphasize his bulk and a large knife to go with the bludgeon that could have been a cutlass if it were a little longer.

I didn't lose him, although I probably could have. Instead, I pretended I hadn't noticed him. I took the next turning and headed towards the Central Plaza and the Public Gardens. It was getting past noon, and I was not only footsore, I was hot. I found a small cafe, ordered a brew and a sandwich, and consumed lunch while scanning the crowd.

Hardbody was there, now with company—a slender male, fair, very nicely dressed in blue silk trou and jacket. Both tried to look as if they weren't following me. I smirked at them, paid my bill, picked up my net carry-all —which was now laden with jars of clet, packets of bone-meal, and a few other odds and ends I'd bought at the various Vikk-shops—and went on my way.

I decided the next step was to pay a call on Master Assassin Fee M'Farr. If something was going down on the

Waterfront or in Fishmarket, he would know about it; and if he didn't, he ought to.

The Guild Hall of the Honorable Guild of Forgers, Assassins, Thieves, and Swindlers—called Fatsos by those who didn't care who heard it—is opposite the Merchants' Guild Hall on the Central Plaza.. In a way, the two were mirror images of each other; most of the Merchants paid the Fatsos protection money to keep the inventory on the shelves and the sales staff safe from mayhem, and the Fatsos mostly kept the mayhem to a minimum because they made more coin by not thieving. Where the Merchant's Guild Hall was large and gaudy, the Assassins' was large and stark, more of a fortress than a palace. However, the ground floors of both establishments were hives of scribes and functionaries, all busily filling out forms and filing them somewhere or other.

I slipped into the crowd and found the desk where a ratlike male sat staring into space. I didn't waste time being polite. I know Ratty of old. He might look vacant, but he was memorizing every face he saw. He certainly knew mine.

"Independent Eye Drach," he greeted me with a very slight inclination of what little chin he had.

"Assassin Ratty," I responded. "I have some information for Master Assassin Fee M'Farr. Is he available?" I slid a coin across the desk, just to make sure.

"I'll see." Ratty snatched the coin and blew into one of the speaking-tubes behind his desk. He muttered something into it, then turned to me and said, "Over there. He'll see you shortly."

I meandered over to the side rooms, where I joined a line of petitioners dressed in everything from Licensee finery to Beggars rags. I spent a few minutes trying to work out what each of the petitioners was after while someone behind the doors went for M'Farr.

At last, one of the inner doors opened, and a youngster pointed at me and motioned for me to come into the Interview Chambers. I sauntered past the line, ignoring the glares of the other petitioners, and entered the presence of Master Assassin Fee M'Farr.

The Interview Rooms in the Guild Hall are stark to the point of grimness—table, two chairs, and a panel on one side I knew was see-through. There would be someone on the other side taking notes of everything that was said and done.

M'Farr hadn't changed much since I'd solved the murder of his popsy Marla Lily. He still looked like a grocer, pudgy and squat, and his eyes were still chips of gray ice in his round face.

"You've got something for me?" He didn't waste time, either.

"Maybe," I said cautiously. "One of my clients has wound up with the Dark Ones."

"And you think my people did it?"

"Actually, I don't," I said. "It's not your style, beating someone up and leaving him. If your people do a job, they make it look like an accident, or they give it plenty of show, to make the point. What I want to know, Master Assassin, is whether some of your younger Guild members might be pulling a little independent action on their own, without your sanction.

"Somebody's shaking down the Vikk-shop Franchisees, harassing refugees in Fishmarket and Industrial Sectors, giving them bad merch to sell, and not forwarding their take to the proper authorities in the Guild for distribution. One of the Franchisees got hit on his way to the Merchant's Guild to complain about it, and I have to think the two are connected.

"I was under the impression that sort of thing was beneath you. Master Merchant Drina Vikk certainly pays you enough to leave her people alone. What's she going to do if she finds out they're being asked to pay someone else for what she's already paid for?"

The more I talked, the more convinced I was that M'Farr didn't know what I was getting at. When I finished, his face was beet-red, not from embarrassment but from anger.

"If someone's pulling something behind the Guild's back, they'd better think again," he sputtered.

"I should have thought your spies would have clued you in," I said. "Unless they're in on it, too."

"In on what?"

I pulled out two jars of clet.

"This stuff is the Vikk-shop standard," I said, pointing to the green label. "The jar with the blue label is what's being given to the Franchisees, at twice the price. If they don't buy it, they get smacked up, and if they do, their customers won't take it. They're done either way. Like I said, one of the Franchisees tried to go to the Merchants' Guild to protest the bad merch, and got beaten so badly he expired."

"Not done by one of mine," M'Farr stated. "Unsanctioned!"

"I thought you'd be interested to know that someone's apparently trying to move in on Guild territory."

"And what do you want in return?" M'Farr said, eyeing me with suspicion.

"Just the confirmation that your Guild wasn't involved," I said, with my blandest smile. "And you owe me one, if I need it. By the way, there are a couple of hardbodies outside. One's an ex-basher I think, big fella, scar on the neck. The other's his bedmate, probably—slim, fair, fancy dresser. Any idea who they are?"

Bodyguards are classified as Assassins and required to check in with the Fatsos before they can take on work.

M'Farr scowled at me. "There have been some foreigners in town," he said. "Shipped in from Pangkot. Devon Delrey of the Bankers' Guild tried to pull a fast one on us—hired them and classified them as Bankers' Associates."

"Really?" I'd seen Devon Delrey at Smokey Joe's a time or two, but he hadn't been accompanied by bodyguards.

M'Farr nodded. "He came around a while back. Wanted to hire some of the Assassins for private work. We gave him a few names, told him the rates. He didn't like them."

"I don't know what that has to do with my clet racket, but I figured you'd be interested in knowing there's a new player in town."

M'Farr nodded briefly. "Thank you for your information, Eye Drach. You can claim a reward at the proper desk."

"Not coin," I said. "I may want to call in a favor soon. Call this an advance on that debt."

That was all he had to say, but I could tell there were wheels turning in his mind. He'd been at the top of the Assassin's Guild for a long time, but there were always younger, stronger types who thought they'd do a better job than he, angling for the way to get him out of the picture.

None of that was any concern of mine, though. I was starting to get a picture in my mind of what had happened to poor Franchisee Yonah. I had only one more stop to make to be certain, but it would have to wait until after dark.

I headed back to my digs. I'd picked up some new plant spray as well as the bonemeal at one of the Vikk-shops, and I wanted to commune with Ficus before I set out again.

viii

I told Ficus about Drushka and her problems while I gave it a nice rubdown and spritzed the extra-fine water I'd bought at a Vikk-shop. The Franchisee (not Drushka) had sworn it came straight from the Upper River, where the water was from purified mountain streams. I didn't quite believe him, but Ficus definitely perked up, turning its leaves over to get more, so it must have been something of a treat. As a reward, I got an extra spritz of pheromones.

"I have to go out again," I told Ficus. "Don't worry about me. I'm not going to do anything stupid. I'll get Basher Bob to back me."

Ficus rustled its leaves, as if to say, *You* always *get into trouble when you call in Basher Bob.*

"I know, I know—he attracts the hardbodies who think they have something to prove," I said. "But this time I may have taken on a little more than I can handle alone. Basher's not a bad sort, just male enough to think with muscles instead of brains."

I swapped my small bludgeon for the heavy-duty baton, the one with nailheads studded into the round end and a nice bit of lead inserted to give it some heft. Like I told Ficus, I'm not stupid, and I knew I might run into trouble, with or without Basher's help.

I switched the blue cotton jacket and skirt for something a little more formal—a black jacket and trou picked out with jet beads and my flip-brim hat, switched my walking-shoes for the boots with extra leather in the toes. No badge, of course. I'm an Independent, one of the very few in Lorr not directly connected with a Guild. I have an Assassin's badge, courtesy of Fee M'Farr, but I prefer not to use it unless I really want to make a point.

I sat in my usual corner and took in roast beast and veg at Fletcher's, accompanied by gossip, rumor, and innuendo. I heard that Kaisrin Vikk *had* been seen outside Jake and Holly's, with much speculation as to why a person whose style hadn't changed in ten years suddenly decided to patronize the trendiest designers in Lorr.

No association with the Independent Eye who happened to have an office behind Jake and Holly's, which was fine with me.

More rumors and rumblings of an invasion force from the south, courtesy of the Autocrat of Pangkot. The price of fish was going up because pirates had been raiding, and the fishermen couldn't get to their usual fishing grounds. Someone brought up the nasty taste of the so-called "instant clet" being peddled at the Vikk-shops. Someone else talked about the funny money being passed around, some of it through those same Vikk-shops, coins that went blank after they were handled a time or two.

I listened, and considered, and put several facts together to form a picture. It wasn't a pretty one.

I paid for the food and strolled out into the night scene of Lorr. Nothing new there, either—plenty of people out for a good time, most of them finding it. Licensees and Beggars, a few Thieves looking for easy cash, while the good folk of Lorr welcomed visitors from elsewhere in search of fleeting pleasure.

I made my way down the line of taverns, bars, and dives to my favorite hangout. Smokey Joe's straddles the line between the Entertainment District and the Waterfront. Things were livelier on the Waterfront—fewer shopkeepers and functionaries, more sailors and Aerial Corpsmen, and a lot more Guards presence. The Licensees aren't as refined, the brew is sludge, and you might come home with a knob on your noggin and a missing purse, or you might not come home at all.

I strolled into Smokey Joe's looking for Basher Bob. I found him at the end of the bar, big and black, nursing an amber-colored drink. Not a good sign—Basher usually stuck to brew, not a fermented jack. I noticed he was alone, also not a good sign.

"Oyo, Basher," I greeted him. "How's business?" I signaled to Joe the Bartender that I'd take a mug of brew.

"Oyo, Drach. Not good." He sounded mournful.

"Why's that?" I took a careful sip of the brew. Sometimes Joe's is worth drinking. This wasn't one of those times.

"Velda's left me," Basher said. "She's taken up with some rich bastard from Striver's Hill." He glared across the room to where his former popsy was now sitting with a crowd of well-dressed folk—slummers, no doubt—come to observe the quaint customs of the Lower Tier.

"Can't blame her for that," I said. I took another look at who had his arm around Velda, who was giggling happily. "Teedo Vikk, as I live and breathe!" I muttered.

"His last popsy got herself killed," Basher reminded me.

"And so did the killer," I informed him. "Velda's safe enough. She's got more sense than to go Marla Lily's route in the world. Just make sure she gets true coin from him. There's something funny about the money he throws around."

"Eh?" Basher gave me a quick look, then stared back into his drink.

I thought about how I could phrase my next move. Basher and I go back quite a ways. Back when I was booted from the Guards and I was first on my own, I got into something unpleasant, and Basher got me out of it. We did a few rounds, decided it wouldn't work, and left it at that. He's not one for Domestics, so when someone comes to him with a family tiff, he sends them to me. If I think a job will need more muscle than I care to give, I'll send the client to him. He's not all that clever, but he's a good man in a fight, and right now, I was going into a fight.

"Basher," I said, "I'm going to need some backup. Care to come along?"

"Where to?"

"Warehouses. Someone's putting the arm on the Vikk-shop Franchisees, shaking them down and making them sell bad merch."

Basher glowered at Teedo, who was calling for another round. "Anything to put a spike in *his* shoes."

I was about to leave when I saw something that stopped me cold. Devon Delrey came in, and right behind him were the two hardbodies who'd been following me around all day.

I nodded towards them. "Know who they are?"

Basher gave them a onceover. "Seen them on the Waterfront. They're off a ship from the south, one of Ishka Kunine's, I think."

"They were on my tail all day," I said. "I led them straight to the Assassin's Guild Hall."

"They're with Banker Delrey," Basher observed.

"Bodyguards," I agreed. "Now, why would a nice, respectable sort like Banker Delrey suddenly sprout bodyguards? Especially hardbodies off a Pangkoti ship?"

"Care to ask them?" Basher got off his stool.

"Not right now," I said. "Since they're here, we'll go somewhere else and find out where the bad merch is coming from."

Basher and I slid away from the bar, first me, then him. Separately, we strolled through the main room, joined forces again in the anteroom, and went along the path beside the quays. We walked casually, in the shadows, like two people who'd had too much brew and wanted to get rid of it quietly. I looked around, saw the big hardbody, shrugged as if I didn't care, and kept going, certain I could spot him by his footsteps. He was a heavy walker, big boots clunking on the slats of the docks.

Various vessels were docked at the quays, ranging from small rowing-boats to single-masted fishing smacks to the large cargo carriers from the southern settlements. Most of them just bobbed happily in the river with one or two sailors on watch while the rest of the crew spent their pay in places a lot less peaceful than Smokey Joe's.

At the very end of the row was a good-sized two-master brig lit up with lanterns. A large male was on guard on the wharf next to the gangplank to make sure no one came too close.

I nudged Basher. "Note the crates on the docks," I said. "I saw the same ones in the Trader Vikk's shops I checked out today. I'd say we found the source of the bad clet."

"What are you doing here?" someone yelled from behind us.

Did I say I wasn't stupid? I'd made the worst mistake ever. Just because I could spot one hardbody didn't mean his bedmate wasn't around.

I turned around to face Bodyguard Handsome. He was about my size—maybe a hair taller—but a lot more springy, the kind who does situps and pushups to build muscle.

He swept his coat away from his hip to reveal a nice, sharp cutlass. The ship guard whistled. More males appeared from aboard the ship.

Basher took a step behind me and turned to fend off the characters from the ship. I hefted my baton. Blade against wood isn't my favorite entertainment, but the nail-heads on my baton gave me a sporting chance.

It wasn't a fair fight, but it was a hard one. I got Handsome on the shoulder, but it turned out he could still wield the blade with his other hand. I aimed for his ribs. He dodged, slashed, and got me on the arm, but mostly just ripped the sleeve of the jacket. I cursed under my breath —that jacket had cost me five silvers!

I gave him a boot in the shins that sent him staggering backwards. I followed that with a good swipe of the baton, but missed by inches. Handsome countered with another slash, then stepped back…right into the arms of City Guard Tommas.

I was never happier to see the Guards than I was at that moment. Usually, they stay far away from any street fighting until the bodies are all down.

"What's going on here?" Tommas bellowed.

"We were just out for some air, and these fellows jumped us!" Basher declared, hefting his own bludgeon.

"Why would they do that?" Tommas glared from us to the sailors.

"Could be because they're off-loading their ship," I said, nodding to the crates still on deck, "trying to stiff the Dockers' Guild, and not paying their import duty."

"Is that so?" Tommas turned to his squad. "Check this out, Guards!"

They advanced on the ship. Basher and I faded back into the shadows to let the City Guards do their duty, protecting the financial well-being of Lorr.

"Well, well," I mused as we headed back to Smokey Joe's. "And they say you can never find a Guard when you need one."

"I saw Guard Tommas in Smokey's," Basher told me. "Could be he's on the same trail as we are."

"Could be this is bigger than both of us," I agreed.

"Could be that you should let it go, Pola," Basher said. "You've got this wild streak in you. It's going to get you killed some day."

"I can't let it go, Bob," I said. "A man got beaten to death over a jar of clet. He was going to report it, and someone got to him before he could. But there's more going down here than a few jars of bad merch and a bits-for-stakes racket. Thanks for the help, Bob, but I can't back down now. I've got some thinking to do."

"Think hard, Pola," Basher said.

"And, Basher," I said, "don't worry about Velda. Just tell her to look right hard at any coin she gets from Tee-do Vikk. There's something very funny about that money, and it's not humorous at all."

With that, I headed back to my digs, Ficus, and a night's sleep. I had a glimmer of an idea as to how to resolve both my clients' woes.

I dressed carefully for my next visit to Striver's Hill and the Vikk mansion. The new skirt and jacket I'd bought from Jake and Holly, their latest style, was cut to show off a silk shirt in a small-check pattern. I don't usually wear jewelry, but I added a real-gold chain to the ensemble, and neat brown leather walking-boots. Very smart, very understated, very Striver's Hill. Not at all what's expected of Pola Drach, who has the reputation of looking just a tad tacky.

Ficus rustled its leaves at me when I put it near the window, where it could get a nice dose of morning light.

"Don't worry," I told it. "No one's going to try to kill me at the Vikks'. Maybe later, but not today."

I packed the two jars of clet—the one with the blue label and the one with the green—into my net-bag carry-all and headed across town to Striver's Hill. This time, the gate to the Vikk house was guarded by a large male in a long green coat, with a head-wrap and a full beard.

"What is your business?" he demanded.

"I am Independent Eye Drach. I have an appointment to see Merchant-Banker Kaisrin Vikk." I peered through the bars of the gate. "I see her pedishaw is here."

"I will inform Merchant Vikk of your arrival," the bearded one said loftily.

"You will let me inside," I countered.

"You will wait!" He glared at me then marched into the house, leaving me out in the street to kick my heels for at least fifteen minutes. The local Guards were on the march to send me on my way when he returned.

"You may enter," he intoned. He opened the gate just wide enough for me to slip through. I didn't rate the full treatment.

At least Kaisrin Vikk was polite enough to be in the hall to greet me in person when I came in. I glanced towards the foot of the stairs, where the late and not very lamented Marla Lily had met her end.

Kaisrin led me to a small parlor full of furniture that made it feel even smaller. She pounced on me as soon as we were private.

"What have you found out?" She didn't sit down, although there were at least four chairs in the parlor, plus two small tables, a stand with a bust of Merchant Olber Vikk, and another stand with small statuettes of far higher quality than the ones sold at the Vikk-shops.

I looked around for a suitable chair, found one that was my size, and waited for Kaisrin to sit down, so that I could. She stayed on her feet. So did I.

"I've found one possible source for your husband's new income," I said. "He's been seen in some disreputable places with your brother Teedo and Teedo's, um, companions."

Kaisrin sniffed scornfully. "If you mean that waterfront establishment called Smokey Joe's, that is old news," she said.

"What's new news is that they've been joined by some characters from Pangkot," I told her. "I've been doing some Eyeing for another client who is connected to your family's business enterprises. Someone is trying to force the shopkeepers to stock inferior merchandise. When one of them protested, he was beaten so badly he wound up with the Dark Ones."

Kaisrin gasped. No doubt in my mind—this was the first she'd heard of the bad merch.

"My mam must know of this at once!" she decided.

She tapped on a door I discovered connected the larger parlor to the small one from which Master Merchant Drina Vikk ruled her little empire. Elder Vikk was dictating something to her youngest child, Betriz, who served as her mother's secretary and general dogsbody.

Elder Vikk recognized me and gave me the Vikk glare. "What is this? Why do you interrupt? Why is this person here? She is not welcome in this house!"

"Mam, Independent Eye Drach has found out something important!" Kaisrin's reply stopped the sputtering. "Tell her!"

Once again I gave the information.

"I have two jars of clet," I finished up. "One has a green label and is full of coarse-ground clet, of the sort generally prepared by straining hot water through the grounds. The other, the one with the blue label, is a powdered form. I don't drink the stuff myself, but I have it on good authority that it is weak, tastes awful, and is a general waste of money and time to prepare.

"Your people are being forced to accept bad merch, Elder Vikk, and when one of them dared to protest, he was beaten to death."

I was taking a chance that Elder Drina Vikk really believed the guff she spouted about the integrity of the Vikk-shops' merch, and how her mission was to provide necessaries at low cost to those who could not afford to shop anywhere else.

It looked as if I'd gambled right. The old female turned red and purple with rage.

"How dare they!" she fairly exploded. "Who is responsible for this outrage!"

"That's what I was trying to find out when I was set upon last night," I said. "I saw the clet being offloaded secretly from a ship that is owned by one Ishka Kunine."

Kaisrin took a sharp breath. "That person has been courting Devon's sister Selva," she hissed. "He is not a person of good repute."

"Interesting," I said. I worked it out for them. "Captain Kunine has this bad merch to sell. Selva has a brother who has money. Your son and brother Teedo has access to the shops that can move the merch."

"He does not!" Elder Vikk snapped. "Who would allow Teedo to purchase stock for our shops?"

"I did," Betriz squeaked. Everyone stared at her. She shrank back under all that ferocity. "Well, he said he could get me clet for less than we usually paid, and so I gave him a draft on the Delrey bank, and he bought it. And I asked Selva if it was good, and she said it was good enough for the Vikk-shops."

"And Teedo bought the stuff and kept the difference for himself," I murmured.

Elder Vikk turned her icy blue eyes to me. "What do you get out of this, Drach? Your fee, I suppose?"

"True, I get my fee," I said. "But I learned all of this because I've been working for one of those Franchisees of yours, Elder Vikk. Her husband was the one beaten because he tried to do the right thing. He cared enough for the integrity of the Vikk name to dare to go to the Merchants' Guild. You could say he perished for you, Elder Vikk."

She blinked a bit. "Such devotion!" she murmured. Then she got back to business. "And what is your part in this, Eye Drach?"

"I'm just an intermediary. But perhaps if you were to reduce the rental on Francisee Drushka's shop as recompense for her husband's sacrifice in your name, that might keep this business out of the courts, and the Merchants' Guild wouldn't have to investigate the sources of the merchandise."

Elder Vikk thought this over for a short while; I could see wheels turning in her mind. She didn't want an investigation that might turn up even shadier deals than this business with Captain Kunine, and she needed the support of those Franchisees.

She snapped, "Betriz! Get the particulars from Independent Eye Drach!" She rang a little bell sitting on the table next to her grand chair. Another bearded servant answered the call. "Munshez! Inform Master Teedo he is wanted here. Now!"

What I should have done at that point was bow out, but I hadn't been dismissed. And I wanted to learn what else was going down in the Vikk household. I just stepped back to where I would be hidden when the door opened.

Teedo appeared, looking sleepy and disheveled.

"Teedo!" Elder Vikk's voice could have cut glass. "You have been drinking and wenching with my money!"

"Mam found out about the clet," Betriz squeaked.

"You bought merchandise without testing it. You inflicted unworthy goods on our Franchisees!"

You'd think he'd been holding revels with the Dark Ones!

"No such thing!" Teedo protested. "I made a perfectly good deal with someone who had a product for sale…" He stopped when he saw the two jars of clet on the little table next to the throne.

"*This* 'product'?" Elder Vikk pointed to the blue-labeled jar.

"It's perfectly good clet, just ground down to a powder so that you drop a spoonful into hot water. It makes a hot drink, tastes just like clet," Teedo huffed.

"Have you tasted it?" Kaisrin demanded.

"No need to," Teedo said. "And besides, who would know if it was good or not? The only ones who'd buy it are the kind who buy our other merch."

"Our merchandise," Elder Vikk said, carefully enunciating every syllable, "is not cheap. It is inexpensive. Do not denigrate our customers. They are as demanding as any of your profligate cronies. You took money given to you for purchase of stock, you used it to get inferior goods, and pocketed the difference. You are a thief! And you are not even a Licensed Thief!"

"Now, wait a bit, Mam!" Teedo protested. "I didn't use all *your* money. I got some of it from Delrey's sister

Selva. It was her friend Kunine who had the shipment. She said it was well-liked in Pangkot."

I must have made a noise, because I suddenly became the focus of attention. I smiled blandly.

"I was not dismissed," I said by way of excuse. "Of course, I will say nothing of what I've just heard."

"You'd be wise not to," Elder Vikk said meaningfully.

"But I would suggest, Merchant Kaisrin, that you ask your spouse why he needs two unauthorized assassins in his household," I said. "And Elder Vikk, I would also consider whether someone who wanted to circulate false coin might use your shops to do it. Now, with your permission, Elder Vikk, I will withdraw."

I slid out the door before anyone could stop me and got out into the street without too much trouble. I went back to the office, thankful to be away from the Vikk clan.

I could report to Drushka that her spouse had been vindicated. I had earned my fees. I filled out all the forms required for Administration purposes. The case was, as far as it went, closed.

x

You'd think that was that. But there were consequences, of course. Nothing goes unpunished in Lorr.

I went back to Drushka's shop the next day and told her what had happened at the Vikk mansion. She had already received an official notice that her rental was reduced by half, and that Yonah would be listed as an Honored Franchisee with those who had been killed or wounded in the Traders' War.

I also told her I'd found out who had beaten poor Yonah.

"I don't know their names," I confessed. "But they work for Banker Delrey as bodyguards. I've already reported them to the Assassins' Guild. They'll take care of them for you."

"They will suffer in the Underworld," she told me.

"I don't know about the Underworld, but they'll get a hefty fine for being Unlicensed," I said.

Drushka told me she'd found a use for that powdered clet. Seems that what she'd brewed up she'd thrown into her garden-plot, and the plants liked it so much they started growing madly. So, she moved it over onto the shelf with the potting soil and bonemeal, and she'd sold almost all of it to people who were using it for their pot-plants and yard gardens. I tried it on Ficus, and Ficus practically glowed green and blue with delight.

The Assassins' Guild put out a Post declaring that *all* Bodyguards were henceforth to be designated as Assassins and had to register with the Guild and pay the fees. For some of those characters, that was worse than if they'd been sentenced to the mines.

Kaisrin Vikk bought two outfits from Jake and Holly and wore them to one of the more elegant gatherings at the Orchestra, with Devon in tow. Banker Devon Delrey was not seen in Smokey Joe's for a while.

I'd done what I was paid to do, but there was something nagging at me. I had the feeling I'd missed something, that there was something else I should have done.

I took my worries to Smokey Joe's one night. Basher was at the bar, with Velda by his side.

"Where's Teedo?" I asked, looking at the center table where Teedo had held court for several weeks. The table was now vacant.

"Teedo's back home with his mam," Basher said.

"He wasn't all that much fun anyway," Velda said, hanging on to Basher.

"I'm happy to see you happy, Basher," I said, and I bought them both a drink.

Still, I had a nasty feeling there was a lot more to this business than a few jars of clet. I was reminded of one of the stories my dad told me before he sailed off and was never seen again, about huge chunks of ice that floated about in the Northern Seas. Ships would break on them, because most of the ice wasn't visible at all. It was under the water.

Whatever was going on, most of it was all under the water. And I seemed to be the only one who was worried about it.

PRODIGAL DAUGHTER

I NEVER THOUGHT I'D SEE KAISRIN VIKK IN THE CHAIR opposite my desk again, but here she was, three weeks after I'd closed the case of her husband's scheme to channel bad merchandise through her mother's shops and marked the bill paid in full.

She's a middle-aged female, this time wearing a frumpy brown tweed jacket and long skirt more suitable to the North Country mountains than the ultra-chic streets of Lorr, twisting a handkerchief in her hands, trying to find the words to explain why she'd sought me out once more.

"I want you to find my sister Betriz," she blurted. "She's gone."

"Gone? As in…?" I asked delicately. There are gradations of *gone*, and one of them has to do with the unspeakable.

Kaisrin got a grip on her emotions. "She's missing."

That was odd. As far as I knew, Betriz Vikk never left her mother's side, and old Master Merchant Drina Vikk hadn't left her house on Striver's Hill since her Dear Departed Olber was laid to Eternal Rest twenty years ago.

"Since when?" I pulled a sheet of paper out of the desk drawer, ready to take notes. If Merchant-Banker Kaisrin Vikk-Delrey was worried enough to come all the way into Clothier's Alley, things must be serious; and when a hard-boiled Conservationist was ready to spend coin on an Independent Eye instead of using the Merchants' Guild Investigative Service or turning to the Admin Security Force, the situation is really dire.

"I last saw her two nights ago. I was summoned to my parent's house for dinner. Betriz was present then. However, when I paid my usual call yesterday morning, her servant told me she would not see me. And this morning, when I went to the house, I was told she was ailing, would not be able to speak with me. This is not like Betriz."

"Perhaps she was under orders not to speak with anyone connected with the Delrey Bankers," I suggested. It was all over Lorr by now that Kaisrin's spouse Devon Delrey was in Elder Vikk's bad books because of his involvement with the bad merch scheme.

"That is possible." Kaisrin took a deep breath and continued. "But of late, Betriz has been going out, with proper supervision. In fact, I saw her at one of the gatherings organized by Devon's sibling, Selva."

There was something the Post Six gossips had missed —Betriz Vikk at one of Selva Delrey's soirees.

"How did she get out of Master Merchant Vikk's clutches?" I ventured to ask.

"Teedo was her escort," Kaisrin said. "He persuaded Mam to let Betriz attend one or two outside functions. After all, Selva is part of the family, and these were not grand affairs, just small parties where poets read their offerings and one of Selva's pet singers performed."

That sounded even more suspicious. Teedo Vikk is known as a lover of things beautiful, especially Clothier's Models and entertainment Licensees. He's more likely to be seen at a wheel race or a basher-bout than a poetry reading or a soiree where someone sings sentimental ballads.

"Banker Selva's known for sponsoring artists and entertainers," I remarked. She was also known for dropping them when they ceased to amuse her. "When did Merchant Teedo last see Betriz?" Getting any useful fact out of this woman was like pulling teeth out of a fowl.

Kaisrin took another breath. "I saw Teedo this morning. He told me that after the, um, recent unpleasantness, he'd taken it on himself to tour the Vikk-shops in person, to assure the Franchisees they are being looked after by their sponsor, and that only good merch would be offered for their shelves."

"And where does Betriz come in?"

Kaisrin sniffled into her nose-wipe. "Since she'd been the one to sign off on buying the bad clet, he thought she should go with him, to show solidarity and support. They inspected the shops, congratulated the Franchisees, distributed some awards for good service to the Vikk clan. Then Teedo decided to give the child a treat and took her to an establishment he sometimes frequents on the Waterfront."

"Smokey Joe's?" I almost laughed. Trust Teedo Vikk to think a jaunt to Smokey Joe's dive would be a treat for his baby sib!

Then I did some quick mental addition. Betriz was no child, no matter how much her mother wanted to keep her in school uniforms. Olber Vikk was gone twenty years, so Betriz had to be at least that, and likely a few more.

"I believe that is the name." Kaisrin's mouth turned down at the corners. "It is not a place where the daughter of a respectable Merchant should be seen."

I had to agree with her there. Smokey Joe's is on the border between the Entertainment Sector and the Waterfront; you could say it's where the Better Half meets the Riff and Raff. The drinks are sludge, the food is mud, and the entertainment, when they have it, ranges from the clever to the out-and-out raunchy. It's one of my favorite places to pick up the kind of news that doesn't make it to the Posts, but it's not a place for a sweet young thing like Junior Merchant Betriz Vikk.

"And she went missing at Smokey Joe's?" That was all too likely. Plenty of bravos and hardbodies would love to get their hands on an innocent like Betriz for any number of reasons, not all of them friendly to Master Merchant Vikk. Females like that don't come along very often at Smokey Joe's.

"Oh, no, Teedo assured me he brought her home," Kaisrin said hastily. "But yesterday, when she didn't appear at breakfast, he began to worry. Her maid said she was not well—something she ate at the low place, but she would not summon a Medico."

"That was the first time you tried to see her?" I made a note on my worksheet.

"It was. I had my doubts about her illness. Betriz is not one to make a fuss over physical ailments, but if she was truly unwell she would not hesitate to summon one of the Medicos from the nearest Dark Ones' shrine. We are generous to the Dark Ones' Temple, and have a Medico who will come to us whenever we call."

"And this morning?"

Kaisrin's expression hardened. "I would not be put off. I told the servant to let me into Betriz's quarters. She was not there. I informed Mam. She was not pleased."

I would have liked to be the lizard in the corner when that happened!

"She blamed Teedo for exposing her to 'evil influences' at Selva's soiree. Teedo told her he had meant it for the best, that he thought Betriz would enjoy hearing the new singer, a very talented young man. Mam was not amused. She has been quite adamant about keeping Betriz away from talented young men."

Or any others, I thought. Master Merchant Vikk was keeping Betriz under her thumb instead of paying some office drone for the privilege of serving one of the richest and most influential merchants in Lorr.

"Teedo became angry, and told Mam that Betriz was old enough to know her own mind, and if she left the house, it was on her own two feet."

"Did anyone see her leave?"

"Someone must have let her out the gate, but none of the servants will say so." She stopped twisting her handkerchief and sat up straight. "I told Mam that someone should look into this matter. Betriz may be in danger."

"Anyone consider calling in the City Guards?"

"Mam will not tolerate the City Guard looking into what is essentially a family matter, nor do we wish to involve the Merchant's Guild Security, which is more concerned with commercial matters than affairs of this sort. We do not know if Betriz was compelled to leave the house, or if she decided to do so of her own volition. In either case, she must be found, as quickly as possible, before the gossip chain starts and the Vikk-shops are discredited again."

Now we're getting somewhere! I thought. *This isn't about a young female, it's about the business.*

Kaisrin took up her tale. "I suggested we put the matter in your hands. You are familiar with our circumstances, you have resolved several issues for us without attracting the notice of the gossips on Post Six, and your rates are quite reasonable."

I suspected the last is what had swayed Elder Vikk.

"What do you want me to do?" I pulled out my standard form.

"Find Betriz," Kaisrin said. "Bring her back to the residence. And do it discreetly, with no public outcry."

"I can't guarantee to keep what I'll find strictly to myself," I warned her. "I'm an Independent Eye, without a Guild to protect me, and I'm only allowed to operate under certain conditions. If I find evidence of crime, I have to turn it over to the City Guards. If I find…something else…it's my duty to call in the Dark Ones. And I can't be held responsible for other people's gossip."

I turned the form around for Kaisrin to sign. "You know my fees—a silver a day, and expenses."

"I will expect an accounting." Kaisrin laid three silver coins on my desk.

"As before, you'll have it."

I picked up the coins, rubbed them carefully to make sure they weren't the kind that turned blank when handled, and added them to the ones in the pouch at my belt. "I'll be at the Vikk house around sundown. I expect to be allowed into the residence without a lot of high-handed foofaraw."

"I will tell the staff to expect you." Kaisrin looked over the contract, signed it, and rose majestically, shaking out her skirts and smoothing the front of her jacket.

"I'll need to see Betriz's private quarters," I warned her. "And your respected parent may have something to say about my invading her privacy." I didn't want to waste my time arguing with underlings while a life might be at stake. Of course, there was always the possibility that Betriz had left her home under her own power, for her own reasons. I'd deal with that once I found her.

"You will not be hampered," Kaisrin assured me. "Good day, Independent Eye Drach. I will see you at sundown."

And off she went, leaving me to ponder the mysterious ways of Fate, which kept throwing me into the sordid affairs of the Vikk clan.

ii

With Kaisrin safely out of the office, I was able to collect my thoughts and go over my previous notes from the last two encounters with the Vikk family. The clan itself isn't that large, but they have connections and cross-marriage relations with almost every other Merchant in Lorr.

Master Merchant Drina Vikkk, the matriarch, the leader, is a fierce little woman who rules her clan with an iron whim. She rarely leaves the Vikk compound. She's always dressed in black, and never spends a bit if she can avoid it. She and her Dear Departed Olber started the Vikks-shops over twenty years ago, kicking off the rioting known as the Merchant's War. I was a tyke still doing my basic instruction at the time, safely tucked away in the Admin Sector far away from all that vulgar unrest, but echoes of it still resound in Admin circles. No one wants to start another Merchant's War, ever.

Teedo is the eldest son, going on for forty, pudgy with good living, amiable to a fault, kicking his heels while his mother runs the Vikk-shops and all that goes with that —buying the merch, arranging for deliveries, hiring and sometimes firing the Franchisees. And, as I have noted, spending most of his time being entertained, one way or another. Visiting the Vikk-shops couldn't have been his own idea; I wondered who had suggested it.

Kaisrin is espoused to Devon Delrey, of the banking Delreys, not the brightest of that lot but good-looking and genteel. He'd made a good front for the bad merch scheme, and was frightfully appalled when he found out his good name had been used for evil purposes. He insisted he'd had no idea his sister Selva's Very Good Friend, Captain Ishka Kunine, had been bringing in inferior clet from the southern settlements and using his crew to force shopkeepers to stock it.

Air-Captain Affrey Vikk, third in line, is a leader in the Aerial Corps. He doesn't live at the Vikk house; when he's not in the Corps quarters behind Admin Hill, he spends his time in an airship scanning the oceans and hills. I once had an adolescent crush on the handsome Corpsman, who risked his life daily in those weird contraptions to keep Lorr safe. We even had a very brief encounter when I did my stint in the Guards; it ended badly. I haven't seen him since.

Betriz is the afterthought, the youngest in the family, still living with Mam, completely under her thumb. When I'd seen her during my investigation into the bad merch scheme, I'd marked her down as a drab-looking office drone, constantly hectored by the imperious Mam Drina Vikk, acting like a scared schoolgirl and dressed to match.

I considered checking for more gossip with Jake and Holly, but they were busy with the fall fashions, and I'd pretty much milked them dry anyway.

I headed for the News Posts at the end of the street. You'd think in a place that practically runs on paper there would be a more practical way to disseminate information than this, but that's the way it is in Lorr. Admin and the Guilds issue bulletins the Scribe's Guild sets up into type and affixes to stout posts set up at key stations and crossroads; and citizens read them or not, as they choose. There are Posts in front of each of the Guild Halls and at the three bridge crossings, plus the ones at the runway intersections in Flatlands, across the river. No one can complain of a lack of information. They just have to know how to get it, and they have to have the impetus to look for it. I knew how to get information, and I had plenty of motivation to find it.

I checked the Posts outside the Clothier's Guild Hall. Post One had the international news, mostly about problems in Pangkot, food riots and religious turmoil, and rants from the Autocrat about restrictions on trade in Lorr. That accounted for the recent influx of immigrants seeking protection and work. Buried in the mess was a statement from Admin regarding rumors of a fleet of ships heading for Lorr, said flotilla to be intercepted by Aerial Corps and Naval vessels of Lorr and turned back.

The Local News wasn't particularly new—the Transport Guild and the Watermen's Guild were still fighting about who had jurisdiction over the Waterfront cargo movers, the Merchants' Guild was trying to stop the Craftsmen from selling their own wares at small markets, and there were new rulings from The Honorable Guild of Forgers, Assassins, Thieves, and Swindlers (also known as Fatsos, but not to their faces) regarding registration of persons seeking employment as bodyguards. Such persons were to be classified as Assassins-in-training, and were to report to the Assassins' Guild Hall to pay the required fees. I had to give Fee M'farr credit for spotting an opportunity to enrich the Fatsos (and himself), but wondered just how many of those hardbodies were going to report, and what the Assassins were going to do about it if they didn't.

The Sports Post had the results of several basher-bouts, wrestling matches, and the status of games players. I didn't have any money on any of them, so I ignored them.

The Financial Post had the usual crowd in front of it, checking the status of various business ventures. I don't have any investments, so I ignored them, too.

My eye was drawn to the announcement at the top of the Entertainment Post. Smokey Joe's was proud to present a new singer, Liko Batom, appearing nightly, sponsored by Banker Selva Delrey.

Smokey Joe's trying to attract attention? Usually the place tried to stay low on the notice-boards. There was a picture of Liko, sitting at his keyboards. If he was anything like the drawing, I could see why Betriz might want to go back to Smokey Joe's, especially if she thought Selva would be there to protect her from any unpleasantness she might encounter among the Lower Tier.

I'd saved the best for last. Post Six is for ordinary folk to put their notices—small shops opening, lovers trying to make contact with each other, personal messages. In other words—gossip. I checked each posting carefully, from the top of the post to the bottom.

There was nothing from Betriz Vikk. No mention of Betriz Vikk. Nothing that might be a ransom note, or a plea for help, nothing that sounded like it came from Betriz Vikk. Not even an anonymous posting suggesting something unsavory about Betriz Vikk.

However, there *were* several snide remarks about "a well-known Merchant seen in company with a certain Licensed entertainer, at an establishment of ill-repute on the

Waterfront"; and another reference to the vessel of "a certain lady of means and her piratical companion" being escorted from the harbor by official ships. Selva Delrey and Ishka Kunine had been an item on Post Six for quite a while. His ship had been thrown out of port? High time. I only hoped Selva would go with him.

Selva has been a pain in my butt since she was a class ahead of me at the Secondary Academy and made my life miserable, holding my father's occupation of Seaman against me, calling me a "generic experiment gone wrong". Life would be easier for me if Banker Selva Delrey was out of Lorr.

I checked the sun. I had time to run home for a brief snack before tackling the Vikk clan. I would probably need it.

I headed for my digs over Fletcher's Food Shop on the edge of the Entertainment District, dodging the pedishaws, bikes, trikes, and handcarts crowding the road, evading the carriers on their rails. Office drones of all genders were on their way back home, some across the river to the Workers' Quarters in Flatlands, some to the Fishmarket and Warehouse districts, where many of the new arrivals had found lodgings.

My normal stride slowed as I approached the row of food stalls, transient hostels, and taverns that lurked in the street behind Entertainment Row. I caught the glint of metal in the narrow space between Fletcher's and the Gold-Bug Gambling Hall. What was a skimmer doing here?

Fletcher hovered in the stairwell. "I didn't know what to do," he quavered. "I mean…Admin badge!"

"I'll handle it." I pushed my jacket back to reach my small bludgeon as I took the stairs to my rooms. I got a whiff of Ficus's "danger" scent, a sharp tang that put the hairs up at the back of my neck.

The door to my rooms was unlocked. I carefully swung it open to reveal a tall woman in a spotless uniform, trou brown with a gold stripe down the side, a white jacket trimmed with with gold braid.

"It's all right, Ficus," I told my plant. "What are you doing here, Mother?"

iii

Admin Security Chief Regina Polaris faced me with a tight-lipped smile. She didn't seem to have aged since I last saw her, when I was being removed from the Guards several years back. Not a line on her face, her hair still the color of ripe grain, cut into a straight bob. Not a crease in her uniform, either. The perfect Administrator, sternly demanding respect. Totally out of place in my shabby sitting room.

"Can't a parent visit a child?"

"You wrote me off when I announced I preferred to make my own way in the Guards instead of dancing to your tune in Admin Intel," I said. "It didn't matter anyway. I still got the brushoff from the rest of the recruits who were certain you'd put me there as an Admin informant. What do you want?"

Polaris scanned the room with a discerning eye and evaded the question.

"You actually like living this way? In this hovel?"

"It may be a hovel, Mam," I said, accentuating the epithet. "But it's all mine. I pay for it with my own coin. I owe nothing to anyone. Now, tell me, in as few words as possible, why are you here?"

"I wanted to check up on your welfare. Your occupation leads you into dangerous territory."

"Such as?" I mentally went over my most recent cases—a shopkeeper who suspected one of his relations working as his assistant of taking goods home with him, (he was); a woman who wanted to know where her spouse was going when he said he was taking his boat out on on the bay (he had a popsy and a child across the river). And of course, the whole mess with the dead Clothier's Model and then the bad clet going through the Vikk-shops.

I make it a point to avoid physical contact wherever possible, and for the most part, my cases are settled without it. I don't carry a shooter. I keep a bludgeon handy, and I can use it, but I really prefer to talk my way out of trouble.

"There are rumors of strange doings in the Waterfront Sector," Polaris said. "Ships that come and go without paying their proper fees. Cargoes being loaded and unloaded, and males being inserted into the population without documentation."

"None of my business," I said with a shrug. "I handle Domestics. Straying spouses, lightfingered shop assistants. I leave the rough stuff to Basher Bob and the highfalutin' stuff to the Brain."

"But you interfered in the matter of Merchant Teedo Vikk and his scheme to place bad merchandise into his parent's shops. There is a Guards report of an encounter on the docks."

"Only because one of those hardbodies got out of hand and beat up a Franchisee," I demurred. "His spouse hired me to find out what happened to him, and I did. I did my civic duty, informed the proper authorities, and bowed out."

"Not quite." You could have cut the chill in the room with a knife. "You also took it on yourself to inform Master Assassin Fee M'Farr of the presence of the ruffians who call themselves bodyguards."

"That was a favor done, with expectation of one to be received." Standard Lorr etiquette.

She tried another topic.

"You are aware of certain…oddities…in the currency?"

"If you mean silver that turns blank when you handle it, yeah, I've seen it." And I had a good idea where it came from, but I can't imagine why someone like Captain Kunine would be interested in undermining his chief market for stolen goods. "I reported that to Admin, too. Once again, not my concern. I haven't seen any notices on Post Three. I suppose Admin wants to keep it quiet."

"The Administration does not want a general panic," Polaris stated. "We have traced the so-called 'funny money' to the influx of persons from Pangkot. Immigrants fleeing the religious and economic disorder that ensues when the Autocrat is foolish enough to disregard Administration orders."

"Pangkot is its own entity," I reminded her.

"As is Lorr, but both are supposedly under the Administration of New Earth. All such settlements are to be organized under the Regulations established at the original landing," she recited. I'd heard the same in my very first history lesson, repeated time and again on Founders' Day.

"I still don't see what that has to do with me." I glanced at the window. It was getting toward sundown. I had to be at Striver's Hill before the moons rose, but I couldn't very well throw the Admin out. "Come to the point, Mam. You didn't leave your snug, safe offices in the Admin bunker to chat with me about my work, or to give me a history lesson. For the last time, I hope, what do you want with me?"

"It has come to the attention of the Administration that you have had an association with Master Merchant Drina Vikk."

"I was hired twice to deal with matters that concerned the Vikk family. Like I said, I handle Domestics. Master Assassin Fee M'Farr wanted me to look into the circumstances of an incident involving one of his people, who was connected with Merchant Teedo Vikk and met her end at the Vikk house, and Kaisrin Vikk hired me to find out where her spouse got his spending money. I was paid for my services on both occasions, as per contract, legally and binding in Lorr. I always report earned income and pay my tax on it. Nothing wrong with that, is there?"

"Master Merchant Drina Vikk has a reputation for avoiding payment on merchandise bought for resale in franchised establishments. The Merchant's Guild has registered a complaint."

"Old news." I waved a hand. "I thought that was settled years ago. Wasn't that what the Merchant's War was all about?"

"I refer to Captain Ishka Kunine, and his ships that use the port services at Lorr. Merchandise is being brought into port that has not been properly assessed or taxed. It is being distributed through the Vikk-shops."

"Smuggling's not my business. Check with Basher Bob if you're worried about rough stuff on the Waterfront."

"There is more to it than that. The Aerial Patrol has noted a number of ships heading north from Pangkot and other southern ports."

"An invasion fleet?" That didn't seem likely. "What are they after?"

"To take from us what we have!" Polaris burst out. "They squandered their inheritance, now they want what we have so carefully conserved! They are Exploiters, using up resources, destroying native plants and animals, replacing them with invasive species instead of using what is already here."

"Not my concern. I'm not in the Guards, I'm not in Admin. I make do with what I can get, I take care of small things for small people."

"You have gifts, unseen talents. You should be using your talents for better things than finding erring spouses or thieving relatives. These are petty matters."

"The only gift I have is to move about unnoticed. And I don't consider making people's lives happier a 'petty matter.'"

"You *are* almost invisible," she admitted. "And you should use this gift for the good of the State."

"If you want me to spy for Admin, you're wasting time and money. You've got plenty of agents and operatives all over Lorr. I suspect half the office drones in every guild hall are supplementing their pay with Admin stipends."

The corners of Polaris's mouth raised a millimeter, as close as she would ever get to a smile. "True. But we do not have anyone close to the Vikk businesses. Master Merchant Drina Vikk tends to keep her dealings private, within the family unit. We can't get anyone near her."

"You want me to act as your agent in the Vikk household?" I was nearly breathless at the audacity of it.

"If you persist in your association with that clan, you might as well turn it to the good of the State."

"If I learn anyone in the Vikk household is smuggling, I'll certainly inform the Admin. Right now, I've been hired to find someone. If I do, I'm to bring her back home. If she's not…available…I'll report it and be done. And whatever else I find out, I'll see that the proper authorities are notified. Will that suit you?"

I stomped into my bedroom, leaving my mother with Ficus. I checked the wardrobe for suitable attire for a night that might include anything from a visit to the Opera to a brawl on the Waterfront. I swapped my dark blue jacket for a neater gray one with steel beading down the arms and across the shoulder, shiny and sparkly but good for deflecting a bludgeon or knife. My boots and trou would do if I found Betriz in one of the seedier parts of Lorr. I picked out a gray felt snap-brim, hooked my small bludgeon onto my belt, and decided I looked trim enough for whatever the night would bring.

I'd hoped Polaris had left. She was still there, glaring at Ficus.

"You are aware of what this…thing…is?"

"It's Ficus," I said, stroking one of its leaves.

"You know what it does?"

"It sits in its pot. It's green and blue," I hedged.

"It is a sensation plant," Polaris said accusingly. "It uses its pheromones to attract prey and pollinators. It rewards its pollinators with heightened sensory nerves."

"I give it food and water. It gives me an edge," I retorted.

"By enhancing olfactory and auditory receptors."

"In the outer cavities. Not the brain. It's useful in my work." Being able to hear a slight whisper, or smell a faint whiff of something, has saved my life on occasion.

"You should be careful," she warned. "You could become addicted to the thing."

"I don't sleep in the same room with it." I paused. "Is that all you wanted to tell me? Nothing more?"

"I had hoped you would see reason, and resume your place in the Administration, but there is far too much of your father in you to expect that. I had hoped the Founder's genes would predominate, but one cannot be sure with offspring."

"Why did you even bother having one?" It just popped out. "It's incumbent on every female in Lorr to produce one offspring, but why choose Drogo Drach?"

Polaris's stern expression relaxed for only a second. "He was very handsome, and carefree. We're all entitled to one moment of personal madness."

"And I was the result, Sorry about that." I put on my snap-brim and waved. "Be careful when you leave, Admin Security Chief. The Entertainment Sector gets crowded about now, what with people looking for dinner food, and commuter traffic across the bridge to Flatlands. Skimmers aren't seen too often in these sectors."

"I can give you a ride…"

"In the skimmer? No, thanks. Far too posh for an Independent Eye. People will talk." Besides, I don't trust those things. What if the electrics fail, and the fans give out? It's a long way to the ground!

And with that, I made my way down the stairs, back to the crowds and the job I was hired to do.

But I had a lot to think about as I headed for Striver's Hill. I wasn't surprised the funny money had attracted the attention of the mucky-mucks in Admin. Admin usually lets Lorr go its own way, as long as the proper papers are filed and the taxes get paid, but currency fraud is something else. No one wants to doubt the validity of currency, especially not in Lorr, where Trade is king. Even Fee M'Farr's Forgers don't mess with currency; they're more likely to change personal wills or make fake stock certificates. Admin surveillance meant City Guards, which meant trouble for a lot of people who might have thought themselves out of danger.

Someone was making difficulties for the Merchants Guild…but why? What good could come out of messing with the currency? It didn't make sense…

But that wasn't what I was being paid for. I focused on my current assignment.

There were several reasons I could think of for a well-bred Merchant like Betriz Vikk to walk out the door, but none boded any good for her not coming home. I forgot about the Big Picture and concentrated on Betriz as I headed for the Vikk mansion.

iv

l looked for a pedishaw, but none were available at that hour. Instead, I grabbed the carrier, crowded with workers going home to their suppers in Industrial Sector and office drones heading for the prefabs behind Admin Hill. I got off at the foot of Striver's Hill and had to walk the rest of the way. The Upper Tier don't allow carrier-rails to be built on their turf.

Individual mansions lurked behind blank walls, with a fancy wrought-iron gate here and there to mark an entrance. The Vikk mansion was built into one of the middle ledges carved out of the limestone on the hill, its gate a wrought-iron contrivance with a single bell overhead. I rapped at the gate and pulled the cord to ring the bell.

A tall fellow made taller by his head-wrap opened the gate and peered out. This was one of the new immigrants from Pangkot. They came cheap, and were very loyal to anyone who'd take them in.

"Who are you, to call at this hour?" His voice held the lilt of the Desert Folk.

"Independent Eye Pola Drach, come on the orders of Merchant-Banker Kaisrin Vikk Delrey. I'm expected." Or at least, I hoped so. I didn't know how much influence Kaisrin had with her mother these days.

The gate closed, leaving me to stew for ten minutes, Then it opened just wide enough for me to slide through.

Nothing had changed. The yard was paved, except for a patch of greenery where vegetables were planted. I spotted bits of red and yellow; something was ripe for harvesting. It would eventually appear on the Vikk table. This was a house where nothing was wasted, not even lawn space.

I was led into the foyer where another servant, in a dark-red coat and yellow head-wrap looked me over with disdain.

"What is your business here?"

"I am here at the orders of Merchant-Banker Kaisrin Vikk Delrey," I repeated. "On a private matter of great urgency. If she is here, she will vouch for me. If not, I would speak with Master Merchant Drina Vikk on her behalf."

He looked me up and down, then went off into the interior of the house, leaving me to admire the pattern on the floor and the carving on the newel post of the staircase until he returned.

"Master Merchant Vikk will speak with you." The servant seem to think this was a great favor.

I followed him through the hallway to the small room where Mam Drina Vikk sat, a small pudgy spider pulling the strings of her web of alliances. The lamps weren't lit yet, and she peered at me through the twilight darkness.

"Pola Drach." She spat it out like a mouthful of bad fish. "You are here again."

"At the request of Merchant-Banker Kaisrin Vikk-Delrey," I told her. "She has hired me…"

"To find where my younger daughter has gone."

"Yes, Elder." There didn't seem much point in denying it.

"Can you do it?" Was there a quaver in that sharp voice?

"I will certainly try," I said. "Merchant-Banker Kaisrin did not think you knew…"

"That Betriz had left the house and not returned? I am old, Independent Eye Drach, but I am not a fool, nor am I easily deceived."

"When did she leave?"

Mam Vikk frowned. "I am not sure. I know she went out with Teedo two days ago to visit the Vikk-shops, to assure the franchisees that all was well, that Master Merchant Drina Vikk knew of their hard work and would make sure they were only given the best merchandise for their shops. I did not order her to do so, but she seemed to think it was necessary, given the circumstances of that unfortunate incident with one of the Franchisees. I did not think she would come to any harm in her brother's company. She returned to the house with him. They dined with me that evening. That was the last time I saw her."

"I thought she always tends to your affairs," I said. "She acts as your secretary, reads your correspondence, writes letters for you. Wouldn't she know she would be missed?"

"She sent word through her maid that the excursion had exhausted her, that she was ill." Elder Vikk grimaced. "I should have known something was wrong. Betriz is never ill. I said so to Kaisrin when she came to call on me this morning."

"And what did *she* do?"

"She went to Betriz's rooms to rouse her, and discovered she was not there." Elder Vikk pouted.

"Exactly when was that?" I was beginning to formulate a mental timeline.

"Just before the mid-day meal."

"And she then immediately came to me." I finished the sorry story. "Very well. I have taken coin and signed a contract to find Junior Merchant Betriz Vikk. In order to do this, I will need full access to her rooms. I will also want to question her servants."

I already had a good idea of where she might have gone, but no proof. A brief visit to a dubious establishment, a notice of a handsome entertainer on the public post? A visit to Smokey Joe's might solve everything…or not.

"Whatever is necessary." Elder Vikk fussed. "Betriz is vital to my existence. I cannot understand why she would remove herself from this house in such a secretive way."

"Young females often hide their true feelings from parents," I said, "However, young females sometimes write them in personal journals. Did Junior Merchant Beatriz keep such a journal?"

"There is no reason for Junior Merchant Beatriz to keep secrets from me." Mam Vikk was absolutely sure of herself.

I had my doubts about that. "In any case, may I be allowed to inspect Junior Merchant Beatriz's quarters? There may be some clue, an indication of where she may have gone, and whether it was voluntary or not."

"Do you mean, she might have been…compelled?" Elder Vikk turned this over in her mind.

"There are many forms of compulsion," I said. "Someone may have sent a message, asking for her assistance in some matter concerning the Vikk-shops. If, as you said, she had been through some of the more…difficult…sectors on a tour of inspection, she may have seen or heard something, spoken to someone who thought they could ask for her help."

"And she would have given it, in my name," Elder Vikk agreed. "Very well. You may examine Beatriz's rooms. Under supervision," she added.

I would have expected no less.

A starchy female servant led me up the central staircase to another hall. I was led to a chamber as sparsely furnished as my humble digs. The bed was a plain iron frame, with leather straps holding the mattress in place, topped with a plain wool blanket. The washstand was simple— a wooden frame holding a bowl and pitcher. The elimination place was at the end of the hall, shared with whoever was living behind the other closed doors on the corridor.

A small desk sat under the window where natural sunlight could fall on it, with a small alcohol lamp to supply lighting for the evening hours; neither electric lamp nor electric outlet in this barren room. It was furnished with the usual writing materials—pens and an inkwell, a small stack of writing-paper, and four ledgers neatly placed in the center of the writing surface.

There were no pictures on the walls, no books on the desk, nothing to show that a living, breathing person had ever inhabited this room. It might have been a servant's quarters.

I turned to the hard-faced female servant who had been watching me. I ran a finger over the desk.

"No one has used this room in at least a week," I said, showing a fingertip marked with dust. "Junior Betriz, or anyone else. So, let us stop playing games, and show me the rooms she does use."

I could almost see wheels turning in the servant's mind. Who was she working for? I wondered. Elder Vikk might command here, but half the servants in Lorr supplemented their meager income by reporting to one or the other of the Guild networks. Information is currency here.

Without a word, the servant turned and beckoned me down the hall to a flight of stairs hidden behind a green-painted door. I followed her up to a large room furnished with square tables and chairs,. Posters showing the sigils of the different Guilds, the various levels of Admin, the letters and numbers of Lorr were tacked onto one wall; a slateboard covered another. The windows were large, covered with rolled shades, without curtains. I realized this had been the schoolroom for the Vikk children. No General Instruction for them!

"In here." The maid opened the far door, to what had been the nursery.

Here was the real Beatriz Vikk—a girl in a woman's body, surrounded by childish things, kept innocent by her overbearing parent. I observed the narrow bed, covered by a colorful quilt; the bedside table with a small alcohol lamp; the stack of cheap mags on the table next to the lamp. I picked up one, then another. Beatriz Vikk's taste ran to stories of wild adventures on Old Earth, or in Space, or in the Interior Desert regions, usually with a resourceful female matching wits with an unpredictably fierce male, whom she would eventually choose for her lifetime mate.

A table under the window held a wild assortment of items—scraps of paper with notations, ledgers, receipts and bills, and a collection of small vials. I picked one up and sniffed. Betriz used a floral scent, sweet, almost cloying. No face-paint, no nail color. Mam wouldn't hear of it, not in a strict Conservationist household.

I looked through the mess of correspondence, receipts, bills, anything that would give a clue as to where Beatriz might have gone.

"When did you last see Junior Merchant Betriz?" I asked.

The servant considered, then blurted, "She went into this room after dinner two nights ago. When I came in to get her dressed for breakfast the next day, she was gone."

"Gone? As in, not here?"

The servant nodded. "And her day dress was gone, too."

"Nothing else?"

"Not that I could tell."

"And you didn't tell anyone she was gone?" I wheeled around to face the servant. "It's been nearly two whole days!"

"I didn't know what to do!" the servant wailed. "I couldn't tell Merchant Vikk, I just couldn't. All I could do was say that Junior Betriz was ill. I thought she'd been to the stables, or on some business for the Master Merchant, and she'd come back, and no one the wiser."

"But she didn't come back," I said. I riffled through the papers on the desk once more. A stiff cardboard disc fell out of the sheaf. I picked it up and turned it over in my fingers. A drinks chit from Smokey Joe's.

A number scrawled on the blank back caught my eye—*10 N.* An assignation? Could it be Betriz walked out on her own, seeking the kind of romance she'd read about in those mags? She might not thank me for interfering with her love life, but I'd taken coin, and I'd do what I was paid to do, whether Betriz liked it or not.

I thanked the servant, and made my way down the stairs and out the door without encountering any more Vikks.

I began to have a sense of what Betriz was really like. She was trapped in that house with an overbearing mam. She dreamed of adventure…

I thought about those mags. Where did she get them?

I was pretty sure Elder Vikk wouldn't approve of such frivolous maunderings, not educational, not promoting moral or ethical behavior. Then I thought about the kiosk at the carrier-station at the bottom of Striver's Hill, next to the News Posts.

I strolled through the courtyard. The gatekeeper was at his post.

"Oyo," I greeted him. "I see you are a very attentive servant to Master Merchant Vikk."

"I keep the gate," he said stolidly.

"And you see everyone who passes through. When did you see Junior Merchant Betriz last?"

He gaped like a hooked fish. "I did not see Junior Merchant Betriz…"

"Is there any other entrance or exit to this house?"

"There is the gate used by vendors and the other servants that leads to the back of the house."

"But you can see the path from here," I pointed out. "If Junior Merchant Betriz left by that gate, she would have been seen, if not by you, then by the other gatekeeper. So, I ask you again, when did you let Junior Merchant Betriz out of the gate?"

He made some whuffling noises, then admitted, "I let her out yesterday, just before the noon meal. She was only going to the kiosk, she said, to get the new mag they were keeping for her. I watched her go down the hill…"

""But she didn't come back up? Why didn't you say something when she didn't return?"

"Because she got into the Delrey pedishaw on her way down the hill," the gatekeeper explained. "I thought she was on an errand, or perhaps it was a social event. I do not keep the gate at night, I did not know she had not returned from her errand or engagement. Do not report me, I will lose my place, and not get another!" He was nearly in tears, all hauteur gone.

I digested this new information as he opened the gate and let me out onto the road leading down to the Grand Boulevard, and the center of Lorr. I didn't know where the Delrey connection came in, but I had a feeling it was something to do with Selva Delrey's sudden affection for the Vikk clan, particularly Teedo and Betriz.

Below me, I could see sparkles where the electric lamps were turned on along the Grand Boulevard, all the way to Entertainment Row and the river beyond. The sun had set. The Silver Moon was risen; the Gold Moon would be up soon. Plenty of light for a trek across Lorr, even without the glitter of the lanterns in the Entertainment Sector. I headed toward the river, where I fully expected my questions to be answered.

v

By the time I got back to the Entertainment Sector, Gold Moon was high and Silver Moon was just rising. The late-summer sun had set, the heat of the day was wearing off, assisted by the breeze across the river. Lanterns had been lit, the electrics were glowing, and everyone was out for a good time.

I shouldered through the crowd of young and not-so-young males and females seeking partners for a night or maybe more, and those ready to serve them. Buskers sang, danced, juggled, spun tales, or just grinned foolishly, coaxing small coins for their troubles. The smell of roasting meat lured me to one of the food-carts, where I got a helping of shaved beast on a bed of veg, the whole enclosed in a half-loaf, and a root-drink to wash it down.

I munched and sipped as I rambled through Entertainment Row, dodging the Beggars, avoiding the City Guards, spotting a couple of Fatso Thieves working the crowd. I stopped to listen to Randi and Kari, male and female, him in a kilt and hat topped with a jaunty feather, her in a filmy skirt and loose blouse draped with spangled scarfs. One strumming a gittar, the other holding a small drum. They sang about a ship that never came back from its voyage. A few folks threw coin into the gittar case at their feet.

"Oyo. How's business?" I checked the open gittar case. A few copper bits, a few silvers. Enough for a week's rent and food, not much more.

"Doing all right." Kari shrugged. "Gotta be careful of coin, we hear there's something weird about silver."

"Good idea." I took another bite of my loaf. "I hear Smokey Joe is hiring singers."

"Only one, and he's new in town," Randi said.

"I've seen the posts. Is he any good?"

Kari shrugged again, setting her scarves fluttering. "I couldn't say, I've only heard him once, and that was in passing. We stay off the Waterfront. Bad things happen there."

"Good luck to you, then." I finished my loaf and drink, deposited the wrappers in the basket for waste collection, and continued my stroll.

The river was to my left, surging to the ocean. Insects buzzed over the grassy spots between the piers where pleasure-boats were stacked, waiting for the next day's customers to take a short jaunt to see Lorr from the water.

The air was heavy with the mist rising off the water, and the reek of pitcher-plants and sundews catching their prey. Summer was almost over, the ripe scent of autumn hung over the riverside.

The road narrowed. A line of lanterns strung across it marked the end of the Entertainment Sector and the official beginning of the Waterfront. The Transport Guild's way-station and repair sheds were across the road from the Waterfront docks. Spare carriers were stored behind the way-station, while the rotary turned the ones still in use for the next trip across town. A couple of transporteers lounged in the doorway of the way-station, taking a quick break before their next shift.

A few more strides, and I arrived at Smokey Joe's, a wooden building with a pitched roof that was said to have started as a simple shack back at the First Landing, when they were building the Landing Operations/Rest and Recreation compound that became the City Of Lorr. Wings and a second story had been added over the years, so now the building sprawled across the riverbank. It was unmarked, shadowed, lurking beside the river. No electrics, no lanterns, just a plain wooden sign over the door at the far end of one wall labeled the place, but everyone who had to know about it did. Anyone else didn't have to know, and it was probably just as well.

No one knew who "Joe" was, or why he was "Smokey". No one was even quite sure who owned Smokey Joe's, although opinion was divided between Admin and the Assassins. The brew was sludge, the food was muck, and don't even think of what went into the jack, but the Regulars didn't care. Transporteers grabbing a brew before heading back to their lodgings in Fishmarket, sailors off the ships on the Waterfront, and the occasional mech-tech out for a night's spree weren't fussy about the quality of what they ate or drank, so long as it was cheap. On the other hand, the ambiance was perfect for people who weren't supposed to know each other to meet in relative privacy. No one questioned anyone at Smokey Joe's.

I nodded to Sneaky Pete, the old geezer who watched the door from his cubbyhole in the anteroom. He looked as if he'd been there since the First Landing, but I knew from experience he could take on a rowdy visitor, or expel one of the Fatsos who got out of hand.

"Oyo, Pete. How's business? Anything happening?"

Pete looked me over. "Been a while, Pola Drach."

"I've been working in Flatlands." I ignored the implied insult. Sneaky Pete never gave anyone their full title. "I hear Teedo Vikk's been around, though."

"Maybe." Pete squinted over my shoulder at a couple of well-dressed types. "Tokens!" he demanded.

I knew I wouldn't get any more out of him, and passed through the open door into the main barroom.

I looked the place over. I hadn't been in for a week or two, but there was something different, a different feel to the place. It wasn't the décor, that was still pretty basic— tables, chairs, a long bar against one wall with shelves of jugs and bottles, and a standing keg of brew. No bright posters selling different types of brew or jack; it was all one at Smokey Joe's.

The beaded curtain at the narrow end of the room swung back and forth as Licensees brought their customers from the gaming area to the rooms at the back. Sex in Lorr is a commodity, but it's handled in private. Some things are best left unseen.

As for the gaming, Smokey Joe's leaves the razzle-dazzle and the bells and whistles to the casinos on Entertainment Row. A couple of tables in the back room for cards, another for dice, that was all that was needed for the regular customers.

I let my eyes get used to the dimness after the glitter of Entertainment Row. I saw some new faces, the sort that usually didn't get past the lights and lanterns of Entertainment Row—a set of youngish males in white jackets and black trou, hair slicked down one side, up on the other. I put them down as Admin renegades, off the leash for a night of wild abandon amongst the Lower Tier. A little early for that kind of thing; they usually descended on the Entertainment Sector after the obligatory nightly dinner with parents. No females in the group, which isn't odd. Most Upper Tier females prefer more refined entertainment than Smokey Joe's.

The sailors in canvas jackets and trou at another table were throwing down brew as if it was the last thing they'd ever drink, and throwing down silver to pay for it; I only hoped it wouldn't go blank before Manager Joe got it into his money-box. A couple of transporteers at the next table were arguing about something, probably the results of yesterday's basher-bouts. Nothing out of the ordinary there.

The ones that had me frowning were the squad of hard-bodies at the far end of the bar. Leather jackets and trou, knives at the waist, and I thought I saw the glint of a shooter under one's coat. They were loud, they were laying down jack, and they were flashing Fatso badges instead of paying for their drinks. If these were Fee M'Farr's new recruits, he was making a big mistake. These characters didn't understand the unwritten rules of Lorr, the ones not covered by the Regs. I could sense trouble, bad trouble, the kind that calls out the Guards. No one in Lorr wants that, it's bad for business.

I spotted my good buddy Basher Bob in his usual seat at the bar, the size of two pedishaws, dark-skinned, bald-headed, in his usual lizard-leather jacket and heavy canvas trou. His popsy Velda, the red-headed Entertainer, was back at his side after a brief excursion into more rarefied company. My guess? She'd found life with the Striver's Hill crowd boring. I could have told her just how boring it was, but she'd already decided to ignore any advice coming from me concerning the Upper Tier.

"Oyo, Basher. How's business?" I took the seat next to him at the bar. "One brew!" I yelled at barkeep Joe.

"Oyo, Drach." He raised his glass in greeting. "Business is good. How's yours?"

"Not bad. I've got a new assignment. I'm looking for someone," I said. "Young. Innocent."

"Pretty?" Velda sniped.

"Can't say. Could be, if she worked at it."

"What makes you think she's here?"

"Word is, she came in once with Teedo Vikk."

Velda snickered. "You mean the kid sister? He brought her in two days ago. They'd been checking out the Vikk-shops in Fishmarket."

"You saw her here?" I took a small sip of the brew. It was a shade better than usual, but that's not saying much.

"Couldn't miss her. She came in with Teedo Vikk and Selva Delrey. She was all over *him*!" Velda pointed her chin at the singer who had mounted the small stage at the end of the bar. "And wasn't Selva mad! I was waiting for the catfight to begin."

I looked the singer over as he took his place at the keyboards.

"Since when did Smokey Joe's provide that kind of music?" I nodded toward the keyboards.

Velda snickered again. "Since he turned up last week with Selva Delrey. He's one of her new projects."

Basher added, "Word is, he's from Pangkot, come in with the Kunine ships. Things aren't going so well there, so he's looking for a new audience."

"Is he any good?" I took another sip of brew.

"He brings in trade." Basher shrugged.

That's always a good thing in Lorr, but I wasn't sure if the kind of trade he was bringing in was the kind that Smokey Joe's needed.

The Admin boys let up a whoop. They'd come to hear him, and they let him know it.

Liko Batom smirked at the Admin gang. The drawing on the poster didn't really do him justice. The cleft in his chin, the saucy glint in his eyes, the twist of his lips —all adding up to "bad boy, but could be good"; absolute bait for a little fish like Betriz. He was decked out in a floppy blue silk shirt, open to show some chest hair, tight blue trou, no neck-scarf, no headgear. Very Pangkoti, just a touch exotic.

He let loose a ripple of keyboard flourish, and began to sing, in a mellow tenor:

> Come in, come in,
> Come in to the City of Lorr, of Lorr,
> It's nothing that you've ever seen before,
> You won't leave the same as when you came
> > in.
> Lorr is a city that's founded on Trade,
> We'll sell anything that's ever been made,
> But you can't leave 'til you've paid every
> > debt,
> And some folks haven't finished yet!"

That got a knowing chuckle and a spatter of applause.

> Come in, come in,
> Come in to the City of Lorr, of Lorr,
> It's full of dark alleys you don't want to
> > explore,
> You won't leave the same as when you
> > came in.

He glanced around the room and fixed his eyes on the squad in black leather jackets.

> If you've got a rival you want to have
> > killed,

Just file for Death with the Assassin's
        Guild,
By the time you've finished every page,
The Victim's dead…of pure old age!

That got an even bigger laugh from the slick kids and a growl from the Fatsos. This character was playing with fire, egging the new recruits on, and even using the word *Death*. Not done in Lorr!

Come in, come in,
Come in to the City of Lorr, of Lorr,
Everything's legalized, even the whores,
You won't leave the same as when you
        came in.

I set down my glass, and added my voice to the applause.

He looked around again and this time he spotted me.

There's the Independent Eye called Pola
        Drach,
You pay her to listen, you pay her to watch;
She'll find a killer, she'll find you a friend,
But she won't find how the story ends…

Wait a minute! It's one thing to twit the Fatsos, another to mention me. My whole business depends on my being unnoticed, nearly invisible. I'd never seen this singer before, so someone must have pointed me out to him. Not Sneaky Pete, I was sure. One of the Joes? I had to find out, and soon!

Come in, come in,
Come in to the City of Lorr, of Lorr,
A peaceful city preparing for war,
You won't leave the same as when you came
in!

He finished with another flourish and grinned at the audience. I didn't grin back. I put down my glass and nodded to Basher.

"I'm going to have a word with this joker. Maybe you should come along, just to keep me company."

I slid off my stool and headed towards the stage. Liko saw me coming, waved cheerfully, and ducked behind the curtain.

I made my way through a growing crowd, more than usual for an ordinary night at Smokey Joe's. Something was definitely in the wind. I could hear murmurs in the crowd, the Entertainment Licensees muttering something about "Special show tonight". I saw one of the male Licensees pass a token to one of the Admin lads, and heard the clink of coin collected.

By the time I got to the stage, Liko was out of sight. Where had he gone? I checked behind the curtain that blocked the stage from the stark area set aside for the performers to refresh themselves and check their costumes and makeup. Nothing there but a table with cosmetics and a mirror, lit by a single alcohol lamp. Smokey Joe's Management wasn't spending money on electric lighting, that's for sure!

I turned back to the main bar. I caught a glimpse of Liko's blue shirt at the far side of the room, going through the beaded curtain. What was he up to? Gaming? I shoved one of the Admin boys out of my way, hoping he'd make it to the loo before he lost the bellyful of brew he'd just consumed.

"He's gone to the back rooms." Velda said from somewhere behind my shoulder.

"I just heard one of those new Fatsos say something about 'fresh meat'," Basher put in,

I suddenly realized what had me worried. I'd smelled something that didn't belong in Smokey Joe's—a sweet, floral, cloying scent. Betriz's scent. None of the Licensees would have worn anything like it; they use musk-based perfumes.

And then I knew just what was supposed to happen to Betriz Vikk. It was vicious, it was brutal, and if I didn't stop it, it would ruin her, and her whole family with her.

I had to get to that back room before she met with the Fate Worse Than Death…because otherwise, she'd have to live with it for the rest of her life. Assuming, of course, she survived the assault. I had, but nothing was the same afterwards. No one had helped me then, but I wasn't going to let it happen to anyone else, ever again.

vi

The back rooms at Smokey Joe's are the stuff of smutty stories and innuendo, some of it true. From the front you can't see the extensions built over the years, wings connecting to wings surrounding courtyards roofed over to make rooms where evil things are rumored to happen to unwary patrons. That's where I was sure Betriz was being kept, whether against her will or not.

Of course, getting to those back rooms isn't as easy as it sounds. The Licensed Entertainers have their own wing, and they have to present chits when they go in and out with their customers to make sure everyone gets their rightful fees. The other rooms aren't supposed to be there at all, certainly not for private meetings between unlicensed individuals. You can't tax private liaisons.

I pushed the beaded curtain aside and strolled into the gaming room. Nothing unusual there. No one being loud or even enthusiastic. The card players were intent on their game, the dicers on theirs. This being Smokey Joe's, the gamblers were in plain dress, no high-binders here. Stakes at Smokey Joe's rarely rose above twenty silver, at least not in this room. What happened in the back rooms, during private games? That's something else.

Three doors led out the side opposite the beaded curtain. Two were guarded, one wasn't.

"Is she behind door one, two, or three?" I mused.

Velda and Basher Bob came up behind me.

"Door on the right is the elimination place," Velda told me. "I've used it a time or two." She wrinkled her nose. "Only if you have to, though."

"Number two?" I frowned at the hardbody stationed in front of the center door.

"Strongroom," Basher said. "They keep the money there. One way in, no way out." And the hardbody male to make sure of it.

"That leaves number three." I stepped back into a shadowy spot next to the wall behind the nearest card table. I discovered I wasn't the only one interested that third door —three of those Admin lads came into the gaming-room, and they had their eyes on it. The big Fatso bruiser joined them, licking his lips in anticipation, slavering to get inside.

They were blocked by the female guarding the door., I put her down as a Licensee past her prime, one of the caretakers who made sure no one was roughed up too badly. She wasn't letting anyone in that door until she was good and ready, no matter who it was.

I tried to visualize the backroom layout.

"I've had to use the place a time or two," I admitted. "I think there's another door in it. Maybe a storage closet?"

"That leads to something else?" Velda shrugged. "Could be. There are a few extra exits, in case of emergency, and one of them might be in that closet."

I hitched my bludgeon a little higher. "I'm going in. If I don't come out..."

"We'll give you a minute or two," Basher said.

I tried to look as if I needed relief and headed for the place where it's done. It was one of the few times I wished Ficus hadn't been so generous with the pheromones. It reeked of ammonia and excrement, and it clearly hadn't been cleaned in an age.

The room was large enough to accommodate a large male, so I had space to turn around. It was lit, fortunately, by only one alcohol lantern. The walls were plain boards.

The door I thought I'd remembered was adjacent to the porcelain receptacles,. Sure enough, it was a storage closet, set into what seemed like an alcove, stocked with nothing beyond a jug of strong-smelling stuff intended to clean mold off the floor. I stepped carefully around the cleanser and tapped the walls of the far side. One panel moved under my hand.

It opened into a dark corridor that reeked of earth, mold, river sludge, and whatever was discharging from the receptacle. Admin Sanitation would scream to wake the departed if they ever found out about this defiance of the Regulations regarding public health.

I took a tentative sniff. I could just detect that jarring note—Betriz's super-sweet scent. She'd either been through here, or was nearby.

I hoped Basher and Velda would come after me and stepped carefully into the corridor. Manager Joe didn't spend any money on electric light here; one alcohol lantern guttered halfway down the hall, making just enough light to see by. I crept through the murk, hearing skittering and squeaking behind and ahead of me. I hoped I wouldn't run into any of the lizards that live in damp and dark places; I hate creepy-crawlies.

The lantern marked an intersection between this corridor and another, that one lit by a single electric lamp. Classy, I thought. At least here you could see which room was which. Four doors, two on each side of the corridor, probably leading to private rooms, and three more at the end. The scent was stronger in this corridor. Betriz must be behind one of those doors, but which one?

I heard moans from behind one door, a rustle behind another. Not my business, I decided. I headed to the end of the corridor, the most likely place for a wide room, one with space for onlookers. Whoever had set this up wanted plenty of witnesses. I didn't doubt the rooms on either side of the center door were equipped with spyholes, for whoever came in to peep at the doings in the one in the middle.

The scent grew stronger as I approached the largest door. I was ready to deal with it if it was locked, but it opened at my touch.

I blinked in the sudden light. Not one but three alcohol lanterns illuminated a scene out of one of those melodramas so beloved by the office drones and mech-techs. The room was dominated by a huge four-post bed swathed in red-and-yellow printed fabric. More fabric was draped on the walls, covering what might be mirrors but which I suspected were one-way windows.

I nearly didn't recognize Betriz. Her face was painted pale pink, with blue around her eyes and more pink on her mouth; decked out in a white gown with a splash of red across the skirt, sitting on the foot of the bed, she smiled sweetly at nothing I could see.

At her feet, facedown, was the body of a male in a blue shirt stained with red.

Betriz held a knife in her hand.

vii

It took me a few seconds to take it all in. It looked completely theatrical, a made-up scene from one of the plays on Entertainment Row or Betriz's adventure mags.

Then, the body moved and groaned, and I realized that if it was Liko, he wasn't finished. There was still a chance to save this mess from exploding into total chaos. I had to get Betriz out of there before those bozos waiting in the game room arrived.

"Liko is hurt," Betriz said in a childish whisper. "I took the knife out." She showed me a curved blade with a jeweled handle. "It was in his front."

I tried to turn Liko to face me. He wasn't bleeding from his chest; he'd been knifed in the side, and not by that blade, for sure.

"We have to leave," I said.

"I won't go." Betriz pouted. "Liko said we'd be married."

"Liko's not going to marry you," I said firmly. "He's not going to marry anyone if we don't get him to a Dark Medico."

"He promised!" Betriz was close to tears.

"Males will promise anything," I assured her. "Your mam and sister will take care of it."

"I won't go back!"

I heard footsteps behind me and turned to face the big Fatso, the one who was eager for "fresh meat". I didn't waste time wondering how much he'd paid to go first on Betriz. I grabbed Betriz's hand and yanked her off that bed.

"Two for one?" He grinned at me. "I'm game!"

He fumbled with the fastening on his trou.

"Not this time." I unleashed my baton and swung for his middle. The baton fairly bounded off him; he'd come prepared for action with a reinforced vest. His trou were leather, still clinging to his thighs, although the flies sprang open, revealing just how ready he was.

I swung again, lower. He dodged, and one hand went to his waist, where he kept his knife. The other grabbed at the trou.

I hauled Betriz another step away from the bed while avoiding the knife thrust. The hardbody was muzzy with jack, which was a point in my favor, and still unsure whether he was there to fight or futter, which was another. He stumbled around while I dodged him.

I heard feet scuffling somewhere behind the draperies. The audience was getting a show they hadn't paid for.

"Come with me!" I ordered Betriz. "Now!"

I diverted the Fatso's slash and swung my baton right, then left, and got him across the thighs on the backswing.

"Liko!" Betriz wailed, tugging back toward the bed. "Leave him be!"

The Fatso lunged, then dropped across the bed. Basher Bob grinned and hefted a sturdy bludgeon studded with nails. Velda grabbed Betriz's other hand. and the two of us yanked her towards the door.

"Took your time," I gasped.

"I came through the cleaner closet in the place, but Bob couldn't," Velda explained.

"I had to pay, like everyone else," Basher grumbled. "And there was another hassle with those fancy-dans from Admin looking for the best spots to watch the fun."

"How many behind the walls?" I scanned the draperies, which hadn't been lifted yet.

"The Admin types, and the rest of the Fatsos?" Velda sneered. "Five, ten, I'm not sure. It's dark, and they were shoving each other around." She looked down at Liko. "What about him?"

Basher hauled Liko to his feet.

"He's still breathing, but not for long," he announced. "He needs a Medico, and fast."

"We can't leave him here," I decided. I peered out the door, looking for another exit. No Fatsos or Admin types in sight. They'd gotten more than they paid for, but I didn't know how long it would be before they twigged it wasn't for show. "How do we get out?"

"There's a back door leads to the riverbank," Velda said. "I used it once."

She pointed to the right, where I now saw there was a doorway leading even farther into the maze of Smokey Joe's back rooms. I didn't ask how or why she'd used it. There are some things you really don't want to know.

Then I heard the one voice I never thought to hear in Smokey Joe's. A clear, cold voice with an Upper Tier accent.

"I am shocked…shocked! To learn there is unlicensed intimate activity in this establishment!"

What was Captain Sara Atterson doing here? The City Guards were well paid to stay away from Smokey Joe's!

Someone had gone to a lot of trouble to set this up. I'd get to the bottom of it sooner or later.

But right now, I had to get Betriz Vikk and Liko Batom out of there!

I dragged Betriz through the door while Basher and Velda dealt with Liko. At least she was more or less mobile; Liko was a dead weight.

Behind us, I heard the tramp of the Guards as they marched toward the door we'd just come out of.

"Over here!" Velda and Basher had hauled Liko to the next intersection. I shoved Betriz ahead of me around the junction to where Velda and Basher propped Liko against the wall. I left her with them and went back to see if we were being followed. Captain Atterson banged on one of the spying-room doors in the corridor we'd just left.

"City Guards! Open up!"

She turned her head and looked straight at me, and I could have sworn she winked.

Both spying-room doors sprang open, and males in various states of excitement emerged, some with trou open and ready for business. Hardbodies collided with Guards in the dark corridor, bludgeons ready, while the Admin laddies tried to scoot around them, hoping to get away before they were nailed and hauled off to the magistrates. Intimacy without payment in a public place is a fining offense!

There were shrill protests from the lads, gruff ones from the hardbodies, and Atterson's voice over all demanding attention. I heard the *thwack* of wood meeting flesh—someone had resisted the Guards for sure. Male voices sounded in the narrow space, curses and responses.

I hurried back down the hall and around the corner.

"Let's go! They're too busy to notice us."

Then I scanned the hallway ahead. One more electric lantern in the middle of the next corridor, not much light to see by, but I felt a current of air and caught the scent of river plants. There must be an open window, door, vent somewhere at the end of that hallway.

"Where to?" I whispered.

"Over here." Velda grabbed Betriz's hand and hauled her along the corridor.

Betriz whimpered, "I can't!"

"You must!" Velda yanked her along, stumbling and caroming off the slimy walls.

I left Betriz to Velda and turned to Basher, who had draped one of Liko's arms around his neck and was holding him more or less erect.

"How's Liko?"

"He's stopped bleeding, but he's not doing so good." Basher adjusted his burden. "We've got to get him to a Medico fast or he's gone."

"He's not dying until he tells me who put him up to this," I said. " We've got to get moving."

I draped Liko's free arm over my shoulder, and together we dragged him down the hall to where Velda and Betriz waited in what looked like another dead end. Instead, there was a quick turn, and we were standing in what felt like the vent-shaft. I groped for the opening and found it was just even with my shoulders. I judged its width and stood on tiptoe to peer through.

"I think we can make it. What's beyond?" I couldn't see anything but darkness, but I heard a gurgling and a rustle somewhere below.

"The river," Velda said. "And the sundews."

"Better than watchdogs," Basher commented. "No one wants to go through the sundews."

"Not good," I agreed Sundews close their leaves at sundown, so we wouldn't be poisoned, but they still have prickles. Velda and Betriz weren't dressed for them. "But we can't stay here."

"I don't look good in trou," Velda complained. "And I didn't plan for a midnight dance in the shrubbery. Oh, well, I can't stay here. Let's do it, Bob."

"If we run fast, we can make it past the sundews," Basher assured me. "I'll shove Velda through first. She'll take the girl. You go next and grab Liko. I'll take the rear."

"Sounds like a plan," I said.

Betriz moaned, Liko groaned. Basher and I nodded to each other, understanding what had to be done.

Velda, with a boost from Bob, scrambled through the vent. I heard her curse as she landed.

"Ow! Those things are sharp!"

Betriz struggled to get away from me. I grabbed her by the shoulders and turned her to face the vent. Basher grabbed her legs and lifted her up to the opening.

"I won't go home! I can't!" She tried to kick herself clear.

"It beats what's waiting for you here," I scolded her. "Get up there, girl!" I shoved her rear and got her shoulders through the opening. Velda hauled her the rest of the way. I heard more crashes and curses as they stomped among the sundews.

"My turn." I let Basher gave me a boost, and I fell outside, right into the same stand of sundews, now furious because they'd been disturbed at their evening rest.

They came to life, thrashing and stinging. One stem whipped across my cheek, leaving a trail of sticky stuff that burned. I'd have to get an antidote, if we ever made it to the Dark Ones' shrine.

"Here comes Liko!"

I scrambled to my feet to grab Liko before he fell head-first into the sundews. The two of us sagged and staggered, making the sundews even more upset.

Basher arrived last, crashing onto sundews now practically steaming in their rage.

"We've got to get out of these plants," Basher yelled.

Together, we managed to drag Liko away from the stand of carnivorous plants. Behind us, we heard yells and curses.

"I think Atterson's figured out where we went," Basher gasped.

I heard a *ping!* then a *spat!* as something hard bounced off the wall on our right.

"Shooter!" I yelled. Had to be the Fatso—Guards aren't armed. "Run!"

And run we did, crashing through the shrubs and grasses, torn by spines and sprayed by spores until we got to a sandy stretch where not even a sundew could survive. We stopped to catch our collective breath. Liko groaned, Betriz whined, Velda and I wheezed. Basher just gulped air.

"Where…are…we?" he asked between gasps.

I tried to judge our position. Gold Moon had set, Silver Moon was low, and there wasn't an electric lamp anywhere near us.

"Judging by those lights ahead, I'd guess we're somewhere behind Entertainment Row. There's the bridge." I waved at the line of lamps off to our right, upstream, marking the way from Lorr to Flatlands. "I think we're in the Artist's Sector. There's a Dark Ones' shrine near here where we can get some Medico help. Fortunately, it won't matter what we look like—the Artists and Entertainers are used to weird-looking people wandering about at night."

Velda and I looked at each other and then at Betriz and started to howl with laughter. We were all scratched and torn from sundew spines and shrubbery prickles. Betriz's facepaint was smeared, her white gown was stained with blood and the unspeakable stuff from the corridor walls. My boots were scuffed, my trou ends were shredded. Velda's skirts were worse.

We looked worse than Beggars—we were unfashionable.

Basher didn't care how he looked.

"Where's the shrine? This bozo needs a Medico."

"Over that way." I waved at the low line of prefabs. "This must be the dumping spot where folks get rid of whatever doesn't go into the cesspits."

It wasn't as easy as it sounds, but we managed to drag Betriz and haul Liko across the sand to the gap where the Artist's Sector started. Some of the houses were wired for electrics, and some of the Artists were busy in their studios, so we had enough light to see our way through the rising mist from the river.

At last I saw the most welcome sight in the world— the gleaming red-on-white sigil of the Dark Ones' shrine, the universal sign for a Medico. It took my last ounce of energy to stagger forward those last few yards, but I made it. I would let the Dark Ones take over from here.

ix

There were two of them on duty, sitting behind the admissions desk—a tall male, fair, middle-aged, and a short female about the same age, red curls rioting around her face, both in the standard blue cotton trou and overshirt of the Dark Med-techs. It would be too much to expect that they would be full-out Dark Medicos; Medtechs were considered good enough for the Artist's Sector, to deal with wounds, dole out sundew poison antidotes, handle violent weed-whackies, and generally take care of small injuries. Anything major would be sent on to the Dark Ones' temple on the other side of the Central Plaza for further treatment.

The male put down the gittar he was strumming and lunged forward to catch Liko by one arm before he fell down. The tag over his Medico sigil read *Matt*. The female, Miri, was already tapping the key to alert the Temple there was a serious emergency and help would be required.

"Him first," I wheezed, while Velda held up Betriz, and Basher grabbed Liko's other arm.

"Names?" Miri was all business as Matt and Basher dragged Liko off to one of the rooms beyond the admissions area. Presumably, he'd be given whatever treatment was necessary to keep him alive. I didn't know what it was, and I didn't want to know..

"Licensed Entertainer Velda Oska." Velda produced her Entertainers Guild sigil. At least she was covered for medical treatment by her guild, and she'd cover for Basher. I wasn't, being an Independent; I fumbled for a coin.

"Independent Eye Pola Drach." I laid the coin on the desk. Nothing is for free in Lorr; the coin counts as a "donation" to the Dark Ones' Order.

"And this one?" Miri took in Betriz, in her stained and disheveled state.

"Junior Merchant Betriz Vikk." There was no use hiding her identity from the Dark Ones. The boffins registered every child born in Lorr, genetic makeup known and verified. She'd be identified as soon as she was treated, no point being coy about it.

Miri looked Betriz over. "What's her condition?"

"I think she's been dosed with weed," I told her. It was beginning to wear off, and the reaction could be anything from a vicious headache to flashbacks. Weed is unpredictable, one of the local plants with unusual chemical makeup the boffins found so fascinating. The first users were Admin types, then it got a reputation as an analgesic. The chemistry seems to work on the brain in odd ways. The stage stereotype in knockabout comedies is the backwoods servant, chewing on weed, drugged into imbecility. They must have used it to keep Betriz quiet for a day, whoever "they" were.

"We've been through the sundews," I told Miri. "Antidote needed."

She didn't ask why. Dark Ones don't ask those questions. As long as we can pay for treatment, we get it.

She led Velda back to the treatment area. I was left alone with Betriz for the first time all night.

She was in bad shape. She'd been drugged, dragged, pushed, and poisoned. She was coming around, slowly, taking in her surroundings, trying to make sense of what had happened to her. I eased her onto the bench next to the admissions desk and sat beside her. She sagged back, nearly falling off the bench, her eyes closed.

"Betriz!" I didn't have time for titles. I grabbed her by the shoulders and shook her awake. "Betriz Vikk!"

"Where am I? Who are you?" She focused on me.

"I'm Pola Drach. You know me, I was the one who found out about the bad clet."

"The Eye?" She squinted at me.

"That's right. Your sister Kaisrin was worried when you didn't come home. She sent me to find you."

"But didn't Selva tell her?"

"Selva Delrey? She knew where you were?"

"She brought me to that tavern." Betriz sagged in her seat again. I caught her before she could slump to the floor, just as Miri reappeared with Velda. Velda'd been cleaned, dosed, and covered with salve against the sundews and spores. She managed a wobbly grin.

"I'm good," she said, sinking onto the bench. "How's our girl?"

"Better take her next," I said, handing Betriz over to the med-tech. "Sundews really got her, and she's recovering from weed. And I don't know what she's been eating, but it might not have agreed with her."

To make that point, Betriz lost whatever was in her stomach by the most direct route. Miri grimaced. A small Shrine like this didn't run to extra help. I guessed she'd have to clean it up once we left.

Basher and Matt emerged from the treatment area as Miri and Velda went in with Betriz.

"How is Liko?" I asked.

"Not good," Basher told me. He frowned at the Med-tech. "I'm going to see if there's a pedishaw around. I've had enough exercise for tonight, and I've got to get Velda home."

He ducked out, leaving me alone with Matt.

"Is he going to…" I left the evil word out.

"The patient lost a lot of blood," Matt reported. "I've sent for a skimmer to take him to the Temple."

"That serious?" I wanted a word with Liko, but it didn't look as if I was going to get it.

The whine of the skimmer put an end to any questions I wanted to ask. Dark One Kelvin strode in, all wild hair and flapping robes around his lanky frame. He headed for Matt.

"Where is the body?" he demanded.

"He's not gone yet," Matt protested.

"I was told there was need for a qualified observer." Dark Kelvin was his usual supercilious self. "A body was reported in the establishment called Smokey Joe's. It is no longer there."

"Reported by who?" I put in. "And what makes you think it's here?"

We'd arrived at this obscure Shrine only half an hour ago, and already someone in charge knew we were here? And with Liko?

"This is the nearest Dark Shrine to the establishment. It is only logical that if there was a body, it would be brought here." Kelvin looked at me again. "Independent Eye Drach? Were you the one who removed the body from its original location?"

"The body in question was still breathing," I stated. "As far as I know, it still is. Am I correct, Med-Tech Matt?"

"It was when I left the treatment room," Matt agreed.

"And his name is Liko Batom," I added. "Transient Entertainer. I don't know if he's registered with the guild yet."

Dark Kelvin looked annoyed. "Have I been called out for nothing?"

"You might as well use your skimmer to take him to the Temple for full treatment," I said. "After I've had a word with him."

"He is not speaking to anyone," Matt said. "I have given him plasma, I have treated his wound with antibiotic, I have sewn his lacerations and treated the sundew venom. More I cannot do. I strongly advise moving him to the Temple."

"I do not transport the living," Dark Kelvin retorted.

"You've got the skimmer,." I pointed out. "You might as well use it." I turned to Matt. "Did he say anything about who knifed him?"

"He was incoherent. Mostly babbling about his assignment, how he couldn't do it."

That was a shocker. Was he supposed to set Betriz up, but couldn't go through with it?

Before I could think that one through, Basher returned from his errand.

"I've got us a pedishaw," he told Velda as she emerged from Betriz's treatment room. "You've had a rough night. Better get home, and get some rest."

"You're not much better," she chided him.

"I'll live." Basher wouldn't admit it, but he'd had his share of sundew, and he could use a bit of rest himself.

I shoved Velda toward him. "Get out, you two. I owe you. It's a debt, Basher, and you can call it any time."

Basher jerked his head toward the two Dark Ones still arguing who had jurisdiction over whom.

"Are you going to be all right? I've lined up an extra pedishaw, to get you and Junior Merchant Betriz back to Striver's Hill."

"That doubles the debt," I told him. "I've got to finish this job. I'm in no danger from the Dark Ones."

Basher and Velda left me with the Dark Ones and what Betriz had left on the floor.

Miri emerged from treatment with Betriz.

"Your turn, Independent Eye. Unless you'd like to wind up on the floor with that mess."

Like it or not, I was going to get fully treated. I was given a subdural against sundew venom and my various cuts were dabbed with antibiotic. It stung, but at least I wouldn't be writhing in total agony until I perished, eaten from the inside out.

By the time Miri was finished, I was ready to collapse, but my job wasn't finished until I got Betriz back to Striver's Hill.

I shoved her into the pedishaw, leaned back, and closed my eyes, I just hoped I could stay conscious long enough to get her home and earn my fee.

x

It was dawn when the pedishaw tooled up to the Vikk gate. I rang the bell, wondering if anyone would admit us. A servant in long striped robe and head-wrap poked his head out and gave a squawk when he recognized Betriz.

"Let us in," I ordered. "Junior Merchant Betriz has met with…an accident. She has had treatment, but needs a Medico. And Elder Vikk should be told that her daughter is home."

The gate closed in our faces. I waited, then rang the bell again. This time, a squad of servants emerged. Two of them helped drag Betriz out of the pedishaw. Two more followed as she was assisted into the courtyard.

I handed the pedishaw driver two silvers—extravagant payment, but he deserved it. Striver's Hill is steep, and he'd had two passengers, neither of us lightweights.

Then, I ducked into the courtyard before the squad could close the gate again. I had a job to finish.

I got a glimpse of myself reflected in one of the windowpanes as I approached the house. I looked as if I'd been fighting reptiles in the desert—a long red stripe across my cheek where the sundew got me, hair in a tangle, jacket and trou stained with sundew and worse.

I ran my fingers through my hair to straighten the tangles. The rest would have to wait until I got back to my rooms.

A servant looked me over. "Elder Merchant Vikk requires your presence," he said. *Even though you look like a Beggar*, he didn't say.

I followed him through the halls to a small dining-room, where Mam Vikk was being served her meager breakfast—toasted bread with butter, a boiled fowl's egg, a cup of clet (not, I assume, the sort sold at Vikk-shops).

She gave me the same look as her servant. "You've been fighting."

"Plants, not people," I said, by way of explanation. "I found Junior Merchant Betriz. I removed her from the place where she was, I took her to a Dark One's Shrine, where she was treated for similar wounds. I brought her home. I've done what was asked, fulfilled my contract."

Mam Vikk dipped her bread into the eggshell to sop up the last morsel of protein. "So you have."

There was uncomfortable silence.

"I will not ask where you found my daughter, or under what circumstances. I will deal with that myself."

"If I may speak..." I began.

"There is nothing more to say. You have been paid. You have fulfilled your contract. That is all." I was being dismissed.

"Not quite," I said. "Elder Vikk, it seems to me that someone is trying very hard to bring disgrace on your family."

That got her attention.

"What nonsense! Why? Who?"

"I think I know who, but I don't know why," I said. "As to why I think so, there have been too many incidents involving the Vikk clan and its enterprises for them to be a coincidence. First, there was the matter of the Clothier's Model Marla Lily, who was introduced to your son Teedo with the aim of luring him into a legally binding union. Then came the business with the bad clet, attracting the attention of the Administration. And now, an attempt to disgrace Junior Merchant Betriz in such a way as to bring shame on the Vikk name and, by extension, the Vikk establishments."

Mam Vikk grew redder with each disclosure. "This is intolerable!"

"It is," I agreed. "Someone has a grudge, Elder Vikk. Someone wants to bring the Vikk name into disrepute."

"Who? Why?" Mam Vikk repeated.

"Why? I don't know. But I have a good idea who."

"Tell me!"

"I can't. Not without proof."

She munched on the last bit of bread, took a swig of clet.

"I will pay," she gritted out. "Your assignment has not ended. Not until you tell me who is trying to destroy me and my family."

"Is that official?"

"Abdul!" She beckoned the nearest servant. "My purse!"

He trotted up to her with a small velvet bag. She took three coins out of the bag and laid them on the table.

"How much did Kaisrin pay?"

"She paid for three days—three silvers."

"You now have three more days. Five in all. At the end of five days, you will report to me. And you will get to the bottom of this disgraceful business."

"I'll send the papers around—" I began.

"No papers. We will have a verbal agreement."

I don't like doing business this way. It's too easy to deny a verbal agreement. Like the old philosopher said, it's not worth the paper it's printed on. But there were the servants as witnesses, and the coin was good, so I took it.

"I will find out who is behind these attacks," I promised.

I was escorted back to the gate. To my surprise, the pedishaw was still there.

"You paid for two rides," the driver said.

"Take me home," I ordered, and fell into the seat.

xi

When I pulled up in front of the food-shop, Fletcher hustled out to help me down from my perch.

"I hope I did right," he fussed at me, blocking my way to the stairs up to my rooms. "You were out all night, and your friend had a message…"

"I was working, Eyeing," I said. "What friend?"

"The female who came last night." Fletcher moved aside and followed me up the stairs. "She said it was most important."

"She?" I tried to think past the fatigue and the sundew venom and the antidote.

"Most fashionable." That would work to get Fletcher's cooperation. He had a nose for money, and someone in fashionable togs would have it.

I fumbled for keys, but the door opened at my touch. It took a few minutes for me to assess the scene of destruction.

Ficus had been torn out of its pot, thrown down on the floor, and methodically stamped into shreds. Stem, leaves, even the roots, all mashed onto the floorboards, the potting soil strewn over them, obliterating the one thing I really cared for.

I sagged to my knees and let out a howl of despair.

"She said…she'd leave a message…" Fletcher stared at the wreckage.

"Oh, she left a message!" Tears ran down my face. The pent-up emotions of the last twenty-seven hours— the hatred of male dominance, the disgust at the hardbodies, and finally, the rage at this invasion of my privacy, all came to the surface; and I wept, unashamedly, allowing my raw feelings free play, forgetting that I had an audience.

"This female…Did she leave a name with this message?"

"She didn't say. She just came and left." Fletcher quavered. "It was close to closing, I was distracted. She left a substantial sum…"

"She'd have come in whether you let her or not," I said.

I crawled across the floor, trying to find some small shred of Ficus, pushing the soil around to make a tiny pile. The very soil had been ground into the floorboards, as if to make sure no trace of Ficus remained for regeneration.

I inched across the floor until I came to the window. There, in the corner below the sill, was the merest shred of a rootlet, no bigger than my fingernail. It was at the apex of a triangle, still visible—the toe of a shoe and, a hands-breadth behind the toe, the distinctive mark of a heel, almost pointed. The mark of one of those improbably high-heeled boots favored by the Upper Tier to show that they didn't do much walking.

I tried to get to my feet, holding the rootlet in shaking hands.

Fletcher took my arm. "I'll put it in a cup," he promised.

"Potting soil." I gasped.

Fletcher steered me towards the bedroom. I collapsed on my bed as he yanked my boots off.

The last coherent thought I had before I succumbed to the blackness: *I'll get you for this, Selva Delrey, if it's the last thing I do!*

PAID IN FULL

I LAY IN A FUNK FOR SEVERAL HOURS TRYING TO ASSESS the damage, not just to Ficus but to my sense of security. I'd thought I was safe, lurking in shadows, not being noticed, keeping my head down. Apparently, it wasn't enough to keep me out of the reach of whoever had it in for me. Bad enough to be visited by Fee M'Farr and Regina Polaris—the Fatsos and Admin kept tabs on almost everyone in Lorr, for reasons of security. The idea that someone else not connected with Admin or Assassins could enter my little domain and destroy the one thing I really cared about shook me more than I wanted to admit, even to myself.

I especially didn't want to admit I needed Ficus, maybe more than it needed me.

I lay in bed and tried to collect my thoughts, but between the sundew poison, the various bruises I'd picked up in the mad rush out of Smokey Joe's back rooms, and the shock of losing Ficus, I was in no condition to deal with Life. After a few hours I stumbled down the stairs to the food-shop, where I imbibed a bowl of Fletcher's fish soup. Then I crawled back up and into bed, and lay on my back, half-conscious, staring at the pattern of cracks on the ceiling, and let my mind go wandering.

I tried to make some kind of sense of the weirdness that had enveloped the Vikk clan. One thing struck me —someone was trying really hard to throw that clan into disorder. First, by introducing Marla Lily to Teedo, setting him up for who-knows-what intrigue when she got her hooks into him. Then there was the scheme with the bad merch, trying to force the Vikk franchisees to carry unsaleable clet. The business with Betriz made the least sense of all. That was sheer meanness, no profit in it for anyone. And then there was the matter of funneling false coin through the Vikk-shops and elsewhere.

The only part of the sequence of events that had a practical purpose was the bad-merch deal, but even that was more about making Vikk-shops look bad than about making any profit on the clet. Of course, it was possible someone made the stuff in Pangkot and really thought it was a good idea to try and sell it in Lorr, where everyone drank clet; but the labels had been printed to mimic the ones used by Vikk-shops, and that meant someone had to have invested coin in the plot. And juggling the money market wasn't Kunine's style—much too subtle, and not enough immediate profit.

Maybe I was missing something. If there was no profit to be made, was there another factor? I didn't see one. When there was no profit involved, the usual reason for people doing what they shouldn't was lust, desire for something…but once again, What was the object of desire? And if people were being manipulated, who was doing the manipulating? Who was pulling the strings on this puppet show?

Betriz was beguiled by the singer Liko Batom, who was sponsored by Selva Delrey, and Selva had been the one to bring the two together. Selva had been the one who introduced Marla Lily to the Upper Tier, too, hiring her for one of her exclusive gatherings to display the latest fashions. And Selva was rumored to be intimately connected to Captain Ishka Kunine…

I held onto that wisp of a thought. Why did I think Selva was behind all the mayhem? I didn't like her, to be sure, but that was personal.

Selva Delrey is older than me by three years, and was a Senior at the Academy when I entered as a callow pubescent. She was the leader of a pack of Upper Lowers, merchants' children trying to get into Admin circles by sheer force of will and financial finagling by their parents.

"There's the sailor's child," she'd announced the first time I showed up at the dining hall at the Academy. And all the debs in her little clique jeered and laughed, and I was labeled for all my time at the Academy.

Sailor? Maybe, but not a common one. My father, Drogo Drach, was the captain of his own boat, a trader and explorer. He'd sailed clear around the South Continent and come back alive twice. The third time, he didn't. To everyone else in Lorr he was a hero, a Master Navigator who'd brought back maps and exotic plant specimens and led the way for others to settle on the Southern Continent.

As for my respected mother, Regina Polaris was on the Admin staff, rising in the Security system, no doubt about her Upper Tier credentials.

Still, I wasn't the Right Type. Honey-gold skin and green eyes are a genetic mix that don't fit any of the standards. Not dark enough to be Mech-Tech, not light enough to be Admin or Merchant. I never did find my own sort of people. I wasn't clever enough to mix with the boffins-in-training, I wasn't athletic enough to chase balls or exchange punches with the jockos, and I didn't have any musical or artistic talent that would get me a seat at the Entertainers' table. I wound up with the Guards prospects by default, and even that didn't work out well.

After the Academy, Selva used her association with the Delrey clan to become a Patron of the Arts, distributing their coin to promote artists and entertainers, people like Liko Batom. She'd taken lovers—lots of them—but nothing permanent. And now her name was linked with Captain Ishka Kunine, which might sound odd; but Selva had an eye for a good-looking male, and Kunine was supposed to be good-looking, if you like them dark, bearded, and muscular.

I'd heard a rumor about Selva trying it on with Teedo Vikk after her brother Devon was wedded to Kaisrin, possibly with an eye toward making a double union between Delrey money and Vikk merch, but Teedo wasn't ready to give up his free-and-easy ways. Then she tried

it with Affrey Vikk, but I knew all too well Affrey Vikk
had no interest in any female, and certainly not Selva Delrey.

If she'd offered twice, and been refused twice, what
would she do? Selva isn't the sort to let an insult like that
go unpunished. Just how far would she go to get revenge?

I realized I'd spent far too much time musing about
things I couldn't prove. If Selva Delrey was behind this
mayhem, she'd been very careful to keep out of sight,
working through minions and intermediaries. If I was going to nail her, I'd have to out-think her.

The first rays of the sun were visible through the bedroom window. I'd spent nearly twelve hours feeling sorry for myself. It was enough. Time to get back to work,
Drach! I still had to make good on my contract with Master Merchant Drina Vikk, to discover exactly who was
behind the mayhem, and bring the information to my
client. Hunches wouldn't stand up in the Magistrate's
court; I needed facts!

I hauled myself out of bed, and went out to get them.

ii

I needed information. I also needed cleansing, clipping,
and coddling. The best place to get all of it was at the
bath-house.

I picked out a new pair of trou, a clean shirt, and jacket, and the appropriate underpinnings, tucked them into
a canvas seabag, and headed downstairs. Fletcher was waiting for me at the foot of the staircase.

"You look terrible!"

"I feel it. I'm off to the baths. Don't let anyone else into my digs while I'm away. Not even if they flash the Admin Exec's personal sigil!" I warned him.

"I'm sorry about that," he said. "But I thought—"

"Don't," I snapped. I wasn't feeling very friendly. Twice he had allowed people into my private quarters, probably after an appropriate gift had been slipped into his hand. You can't trust anyone in Lorr, certainly not when coin is involved.

The baths are the one place in Lorr where gender differences are observed, and males and females have separate facilities. I've been told the male baths feature cold pools as well as warm, and the operatives will train bathers in physical defense methods, martial arts, and the like. On the other hand, the female section of the baths has luxurious hot pools, masseuses who will soothe muscle spasms, and experts who can make even a faded blonde like me look reasonably attractive.

My bath-house of choice is the one on Painter's Alley, just behind Entertainer's Row. It's financed jointly by the Entertainers and Craftsmen's guilds, and technically, I shouldn't be allowed in; but I slip the management a coin or two, for which I get to use the water-pumps and the pool. For a few more coins I get hairdressing and nail-clipping.

The Entertainers' Bath-house isn't as lavish as the Alhambra Palace at the base of Arriver's Hill, nor is it as family-oriented as the one on Market Road between Industrial and Fishmarket sectors. I wouldn't be bothered with a bunch of Mother's Guild females and their charges, and I wouldn't have to listen to elderly Upper Tier types grousing about their ailments and servants. It's where the Entertainers can let their hair down, literally and figuratively, and it's a great place for hearing the worst about the best people in Lorr.

I paid my usual fee when I entered, dropped my clean clothes in one of the spare cabinets, and headed for the showers, where I sluiced off the last of the sundew venom and whatever I had picked up in the back corridors at Smokey Joe's. Then I wrapped a bathsheet around my torso, slipped on the disposable undies provided by the management for sanitary purposes, and headed for the pool. I wanted a good soak. Besides, if anyone had anything to say, that's where they'd be saying it.

The pool wasn't crowded, but there were a number of females near the shallow end. I slid into the heated water, not so close to the chattering group as to encroach but near enough so I could hear the conversation. I closed my eyes, and gave every indication of blissing out in the warmth of the bath. It really didn't matter; no one noticed me anyway.

"Did you hear what happened at Smokey Joe's?"

I linked the voice to a blond beauty relaxing a foot away from me.

"Poor Liko!" That was a buxom brunette I'd seen several times at the dance hall. She had a wicked kick, too. "Knifed, I heard. Someone got him to the Dark Ones, but it was too late."

"He should have known better than to mock the Assassins." A higher voice, shriller, straight out of Flatlands by the sound of her.

"Was that why he was knifed? I thought it was because of…"

"Oh, no, not at all. She hadn't even come into the place yet."

"But she's got an in with them." The shrill one with the Flatland accent again. "And I heard she's bedding Captain Kunine."

The trio giggled over that pairing.

"Has it been posted yet?" another voice chimed in, more refined. Industrial, not Merchant, not quite Upper Lower Tier, but working on it.

"Selva or the knifing?"

More giggles.

"You know the Guards. They never say anything." The brunette's alto again. "Captain Atterson's gone mute. Probably paid to keep mum."

"By who?" Friend Flatlands.

"I heard the fracas was about some Admin deb who got into Smokey's and didn't like what happened there." The second voice, salty and snide. "She should have known better than to go slumming. Admin should stick to their high hill."

"I heard she was being handed to the Assassins." Flatlands again. "That's just not right, muscling in on our territory. Trying to give away what we charge for, and to the Assassins, too."

"The Assassins are getting mean," the Industrial voice said. "The new ones, they seem to think that sigil entitles them to anything they want. Grabby, that's what they are."

"That's the way it is with Pangkoti," the third female sighed. "They don't know Lorr regs."

"Or if they do, they don't think it means them," the low-voiced brunette added. "What could Guildmaster M'Farr be thinking, to let those hooligans in?"

"Probably had no choice," shrill voice said. "I hear Admin is allowing all sorts of favors to Pangkoti crews. Something to do with grain shipments."

"That don't mean we have to put up with grabby Assassins." Flatlands sounded resentful.

"What can we do about it? Complain to Fee M'Farr?" Scornful laughter from the rest.

I chewed on this as I sloshed out of the pool and headed for the salon, where I got the full treatment—hair, fingers, toes, all clipped and shaped while I listened to the chatter around me.

More of the same. Resentment over the new Fatsos, regret about the demise of Liko Batom, but not a word about Betriz Vikk. At least I'd succeeded in one part of my contract. There hadn't been any gossip linking the Vikk clan to the killing.

By the time I left, I was in a much better frame of mind. I had a good lead, and I looked a lot nicer than I had for many days.

I also had a job to do, a contract to fulfill, and a debt to collect. I intended to do all three.

iii

It was nearly noon by the time I got out of the baths. I squinted in the bright sunlight, no clouds in the sky,

167

the heat of the day radiating from the pavement underfoot. I thought about food, then decided to keep moving. I had places to go, things to do, and I had to get them done before dark settled on Lorr.

I dropped my stained garb at the cleaners and headed for Clothier's Alley. I hadn't been to my office in many days, and I needed to catch up on various matters besides the tangled lives of the Vikk clan.

Jake and Holly greeted me with cries of horror at my appearance—the best efforts of the salon operative couldn't hide the bruises left by the encounter with the sundews, and I still had a burn slash across my cheek. My hair had been brought under some control, but I still looked the way I felt—terrible.

"Where have you been!" Jake scolded me. "We've had all sorts of people asking after you."

"Including the Guards?" That didn't worry me particularly. I had every intention of getting my information to them, just not until I was sure of what I knew, and how it tied together with what I suspected.

"Worse! There was some Admin functionary wanted to see your office. We told her you were not available." Holly exclaimed over the condition of my jacket, not one of my best, a little shabby around the cuffs and collar. "You can't go out in public like that! We have a reputation to consider!"

"This Admin…female? Tall, classy, remote?" Polaris, I decided.

"You know her?" Jake asked.

"Family," I said. "You didn't let her into my office."

I don't keep much in there, but as an Independent, I don't have access to any of the Guild connections to the Big Black Box, so I have to keep my case notes in writing, on paper, filed in the bottom drawer of my desk. Not very efficient, but usually effective.

"We did not." Holly said. "It's locked, and it's been that way for days."

"Thanks." I unlocked the door and checked the various bits and pieces of fluff I'd placed in strategic locations. Nothing had been tampered with that I could tell.

I found the contract Kaisrin had signed, folded it in with another blank one for Mam Drina Vikk's official signature, and put both in my inside jacket pocket. I took my small spare bludgeon from behind the cabinet, where I keep it just in case I need it for an unruly client.

I sat at my desk for a few moments, plotting the next moves. I was almost certain Selva Delrey was at the bottom of this mess the Vikks had got into, but I had to make sure someone else wasn't involved. That would involve two visits to persons who might not be ready to talk to me…unless they wanted to make sure I wouldn't go after them.

I closed my eyes and lined out a possible strategy. I'm not the sort of fool who goes after a dangerous person without some idea of backup. Between the Guards and the Vikk functionaries, I'd be sure to have some followers. I just hoped they wouldn't trip over each other while they were chasing me. I also had an idea how I might get the Fatsos in the mix, too,

I twitched my jacket into place, hooked the bludgeon onto my belt, and set out.

iv

I headed towards Central Plaza, where the Guild Houses loom over the rest of the city, four or five stories high instead of the usual two or, if the owner was really affluent, three. The Merchants' Guild dominates, its dome glittering with specks of mica that hold flakes of pure gold. The Clothier's and Craftsmen's guilds flank the Merchants', since the three work closely together, Clothiers and Craftsmen providing the wares the Merchants sell. There is always friction among them regarding prices and standards, with Merchants complaining about shoddy wares and Clothiers and Craftsmen protesting Merchants' lowballing them on price and hiking rates to consumers. On the whole, though, the system works well enough to keep everyone fed and occupied. Plenty of work for the office drones of all three Guilds.

Next around the plaza are the Builders, the Transporters, and the Scribes; across from them, the Entertainers' Guild Hall, rivaling the Merchants for colorful exterior and lavish furnishings. Finally, all alone, faced with dark stone, the Guild of Forgers, Assassins, Thieves, and Swindlers, referred to as the Fatsos, but not out loud. Not with the new hardbodies on the loose.

The Assassins' Guild House has its share of office drones, mostly mousy little males who lurk in corners and flashy-looking females, Entertainers past their prime. When I approached the entrance, I noted more of the new membership—sunburnt and hard-featured, wearing leather

170

caps over close-cropped hair, arms bared to show tattoos,
Definitely Pangkoti, since no Lorran would mark themselves so permanently. What happens when the fashion
changes? You can't get rid of those markings easily, not
without a lot of pain; and fashionable Lorrans aren't all
that ready to endure a lot of pain for the sake of fashion..

I found Ratty, the gatekeeper to Fee M'Farr's private
sanctum, paid the requisite coin, and eventually was shown
into one of the audience rooms. Fee M'Farr stormed into
the room, looking less like a well-fed grocer and more like
the killer he'd always been. He didn't bother with the usual
"How's business?" niceties.

"Is this about that mess at Smokey Joe's?"

"It was your people started it," I said. "I was there on
a rescue mission. I got a female out before one of them
could force her into nonconsensual intimacy." It sounded nicer than "rape", but it meant the same. "And there
was a singer in the room. He'd been attacked. Maybe one
of your new recruits didn't like his voice?"

"I didn't sanction the killing," M'Farr protested. "But
some of these people from the south take their position
very seriously. They have a code of honor. I've heard the
song about the City of Lorr. It criticized the Assassin's
Guild."

"The song wasn't that bad," I said. "I was mentioned
in it, too, and I didn't feel impelled to silence the singer."

"I've squared it with Admin and the magistrates, I've
called a meeting of the new recruits and explained the
regs. What else can I do?" M'Farr whined.

"Rein them in?" I didn't want to suggest that Master Assassin Fee M'Farr was losing his grip on the Assassin's Guild. If there was going to be a succession war, I wanted to be well out of sight while things were settled. "Or cut a deal with Ishka Kunine. They answer to him, in the long run."

M'Farr grimaced. "If that's all you have, you're wasting my time and yours. Kunine's being dealt with, although not by me. His fleet's being pounded by the Aerial Corps even as we speak."

"Who's winning?" I'd read the posts, but they were usually at least a day after the fact, and contained only what Admin wanted us to know. I was sure M'Farr had a contact in Admin who would be able to get current info from the techs in charge of comm-units. The rest of us had to wait until notices went up.

"So far, we are." M'Farr allowed himself a smug grin. Then he got serious again. "You didn't come here to tell me what I already know, Drach, and the business at Smokey Joe's has been dealt with. So, why bother me now?"

"I came here to find out if one of those new recruits came after me, didn't find me home, and took it out on my furnishings. Particularly, my plant."

"What?" M'Farr was definitely surprised.

"It took me a while to get back to my digs after I returned the female in question to her loving family," I explained. "And when I did, I found my plant on the floor, smashed and stomped on. I don't go around giving my home base info to everyone I meet, so the only ones who know where I lay my head are you, the tax drones in Admin, and one or two very close friends.

"The tax collector hasn't been around for a while, and none of my friends has it in for Ficus. That leaves you. Master Assassin Fee M'Farr, did you tell one of those new recruits to take his displeasure at being interrupted in exercising his male rights over an unwilling female out on an innocent plant?"

M'Farr's face had grown redder as my voice rose with each word.

"Why in the name of death and destruction would I do that? You're a good source, Drach. You've done right by me, I do right by you. Sure, I know where you live, I've seen how you care for that plant, but I swear, by the bones of Founder Fergus MacFarlaine, I never sent anyone to your digs, and I never told anyone to mess with that plant."

I considered for a long moment. Invoking one of the Founders was about as serious as you get in Lorr.

"I didn't think you had, but I have to be sure before I tackle the one who did." I gave M'Farr one piece of information to chew on. "I can't tell you more—you know how my business works—but I can tell you this. I'm beginning to think this whole mess is personal, not business or trade-related. Someone's out to take down one of the Merchant families, one that spends a good chunk of coin keeping the Assassins' Guild going. It's in your interest to stop it."

"That's all you have?" M'Farr wasn't going to let me off that easily.

"It's all I can tell you right now. I've got some more Eyeing to do before I get enough to take to the Admin magistrates."

"You know who it is?"

"I suspect, but no proof."

"High-up?" M'Farr hinted.

"Striver's Row, top tier," I said with a curt nod. "You figure it out."

"Why?"

"That's the question, isn't it?"

M'Farr grunted. "I know you, Drach. You won't stop until you've got all the answers."

"When I get them, I'll be sure to let you know what I find out. Good luck with your new recruits."

I took my leave then , certain I had dropped enough for M'Farr to assign someone to follow me.

I could have taken the carrier to my next stop. Instead, I sauntered across the Central Plaza to give whoever M'Farr had assigned to tail me plenty of time to catch up. I spotted him almost as soon as I passed from Central Plaza to Grand Boulevard, reflected in the window of one of the shops. Fee had sent one of his youngsters, a gangly male in a multi-colored kilt and jacket, the hot outfit with the kids in the Academy these days. I was pretty sure there was someone else, less noticeable, following *him*.

It didn't matter either way, as long as someone knew where I was. I didn't think anyone was out to stop me permanently—not yet—but it was always a good idea to have backup handy.

The Central Guard House is at the bottom of Admin Hill, where the Grand Boulevard ends, a three-story block of solid brick and stone surrounded by a wide swath of paved road. There's nowhere to run or hide, just a blank wall pierced with narrow barred windows. A few vendors had set up food-carts across from the entrance for the convenience of Guards off-duty, and there was a row of pedishaws whose drivers squatted in the shade of the few spindly cycads that grew along the edge of the street. The hillside behind the Guard House had been cleared of plants. The City Guards don't rely on sundews for protection; they had plenty of live humans to do that.

I approached the sentry at the door with an air of supplication, just a citizen imploring the Admin for assistance.

"I have a message for Guards Captain Sara Atterson," I explained after I'd been asked for my sigil and produced none. I didn't want to flaunt the one I had from Fee M'Farr unless I had to. "Regarding a certain incident on the Waterfront."

It took a while, and the exchange of a coin or two, but I was handed over to one of the tougher-looking veterans who kept watch inside, who took me through the building and up a flight of stairs to a small office.

He banged on the door. "Someone to see you, Cap. Says she's got information about the mess at Smokey Joe's."

"Pola Drach? I've been waiting for you to show up." Atterson's jacket was slightly creased, her hair straggled out of its usual tight bun at the nape of her neck, and she had a small trace of clet on her upper lip, all evidence of inner agitation. She nodded toward a small stool next to her desk. I sat, and the two of us had a staring contest, which I broke.

"I was delayed," I said. "A small matter of home invasion. Someone broke into my digs yesterday and trashed my plant."

"If you want to register a complaint, there's a form you can fill out."

"For all the good it will do?" I shrugged. "I just wanted to know whether you sent them."

"You think it was one of my people?" She frowned. "Why?"

"You tell me."

Atterson sighed. "I've got better things to do than hassle characters like you. Wasn't it enough that I stalled those hardbodies long enough for you and your pals to get that female out of there?"

"You knew it was me?"

"I'm not completely blind, Drach. Who else could convince the Big Black Basher to rescue some nitwit who got herself in over her head? And dragging the redhead as well? Why didn't you leave your calling card while you were at it? It was all I could do to keep those Pangkoti hardbodies from chasing you down as soon as you got out of that bedroom. As it was, once I got the Admin lads clear, they went through the halls with their shooters out."

"I suppose I owe you for that," I said, grudgingly. "We found the vent, fell into the sundews, and got the two civilians to a Dark Ones' shrine. By now you should have the Dark Ones' report on what happened there."

Atterson wasn't finished with her rant. "The Admin high-ups have been on my back for involving their precious lads in a sordid affair on the Waterfront."

"Whose bright idea was it for them to go there in the first place?" Most Admin lads and debs head for the bright lights when they go to Entertainment Row. Smokey Joe's isn't on their usual rounds.

"No one seems to know. The word went out there was 'something special', and one of the lads led the pack to see the fun and games."

I thought that over. "Could it have been one of the younger Delreys?"

Atterson's eyes narrowed. "Devon Delrey's been seen at Smokey Joe's, and so has his sister Selva, but they weren't there last night. The youngest Delrey is Gorgeous Gyorgi, the baby of the family. He's at the Academy, finishing his term of instruction before going into the bank. He wasn't in the lot that I picked up, but he could have been the one who sent them there."

"Selva's been linked to Captain Ishka Kunine," I pointed out. "She may not be welcome at the Vikk mansion, but her doors are open to any good-looking young male, especially those with connections to the Upper Tier."

"You could say she's an equal opportunity female." Atterson grinned.

I shrugged. "So, I suppose I should be grateful you made the escape easy? I've got a sundew burn on my face, and my trou and jacket are going to need a lot of soaking before I can wear them again."

"Send the bill to whoever hired you to get that female out of there." Atterson continued to smirk.

"You don't know who she was?" That seemed unlikely. "Then how did you know there was unlicensed intimacy going on?"

"Information received." The standard answer. "A messenger came to the Guard House with word something was going down at Smokey Joe's, that there was illicit intimacy—"

"Call it by its right name—rape!"

Atterson nodded. "As you say. "

I frowned. "The word came here? Not to the Waterfront Guardhouse? Someone must have wanted the top of the crop on hand as witnesses."

Atterson acknowledged the compliment. "I don't usually go on that kind of raid, but nonconsensual intimacy can't be ignored, even if it involves the Assassin's Guild. I suppose those new recruits hadn't been given the usual lecture before they were let loose in Lorr—Do what you like, but pay for it. Fee M'Farr usually keeps his people in line."

"They're from Pangkot," was the best explanation I could come up with. "And so you arrived, but the crime hadn't been committed, not yet. Someone's timing was off. I think you were supposed to walk in on the action and arrest everyone, including the victim."

Atterson said slowly, "You know, Drach, I wasn't supposed to be on duty last night. Harry Goff was, but he must have got some bad fish with his evening meal. He came in looking green around the gills, insisted he could work, but after he lost the fish twice, he was sent to the Dark Ones, and I got called in to take his shift."

"Goff? Isn't he hooked into the Delrey clan?"

"His mother was a Delrey. If he'd caught the call…"

"He'd have been in place to cover up for his peers and be shocked when the name of the victim is 'leaked' to the Posts.."

"And that victim is…?" Atterson wouldn't let it go.

"I can't tell you. Client privilege. All I can say is, check on Striver's Hill."

"Oh, I will," Atterson said. "Meantime, what can you tell me about the singer you hauled off with you and dragged into the Dark Ones' shrine. And don't tell me you can't tell me his name, because it's registered at the shrine."

"Liko Batom," I said. "A clever fellow, good voice, very good-looking. A pity about him. I heard he didn't make it to the temple."

"Died on his way there. He bled out internally before they could get him to the Medicos. Very unpleasant." She consulted a form in front of her. "According to the Dark Ones at the Central Temple, he probably got hit just before we arrived."

"Did any of the eager audience see who did it?" If one of them identified Betriz, both of us were in deep excrement.

"Shades were down on the peepholes in the observation rooms," Atterson said. "I think the idea was to make

sure everyone paid before they opened the shutters to give
the lads a view of the action. One of them admits to hearing some kind of scuffle. Says the female called Liko Batom
by name and gave a squeak or squeal. Then there was an
interruption—"

"Maybe when the hardbody who did the deed turned
up to take over from Liko," I said, trying to piece it all together. "But no one actually saw anything"

"Nothing they'd swear to in front of the Magistrate."
Atterson squinted at me. "Now will you tell me who the
prospective victim was? If she'd been attacked, she'd have
a good reason to fight back. We found a bloody knife at
the scene."

"Details on that form?" I eyed the paper on the desk.
"But you can't show it to me."

"Certainly not! It's Guards business, nothing to be
shared with an Independent Eye."

We sat there for a long minute, staring at each other.
Then…

"Didn't I just hear someone call you?" I suggested.
"I'll stay here while you deal with whatever…"

"I'll check," Atterson said. "When I come back, I want
to see that report just the way I left it."

She nodded briefly as she strode out. I reached across
the desk and scanned the report. I ignored the Dark Ones'
gobbledegook and focused on the diagram showing exactly where the knife went in. As far as I could tell, the
fatal wound had been caused by a sharp blade entering
from the rear right. I shoved the paper back as Atterson
returned.

"I can tell you right now the victim didn't kill Liko. She had blood on the front of her dress, but if he was knifed in the back, she didn't do it. She'd have to have arms like one of those weird mountain beasts to reach around to stab a man in the back when he's facing her.

"When I got there, he was at her feet, and she was gripping a fancy dagger—looked like one of those ornaments from Pangkot, not something that would actually be used for killing. And it didn't have blood on the blade, only where she'd grabbed it by the handle."

"Name?" Atterson still wouldn't let go.

"You mean you haven't matched the fingerprints on the knife to the Big Black Box records yet?" Every birth in Lorr gets registered, ever since Number One after the Landing, and it all goes into the boffin's Big Black Box along with fingerprints.

"We got prints, but the Admin boffins are being cagey about whose they are. So, Drach, I've given you something, now you give me something." As it always does, one hand washes the other in Lorr.

"I've heard unpleasant things about the Vikk clan," I said. I didn't want to give it all away, but I owed Atterson something. "That they deal in false coin, and there was just an uproar over some vile stuff that was being sold in the name of clet."

"I know all about the funny money," Atterson said. "And our boffins took the bad clet apart and decided it comes from the deserts near Pangkot. Come on, Drach. Names!"

"If I give up my client's names, it's the end of my career as an Independent Eye," I protested. "The best I can do is point you in a direction, the same as you pointed me. And for what it's worth, I'll add this—those hard-bodies were brought in by Ishka Kunine, and answer to him, not to Fee M'Farr."

"So I've heard," Atterson said. "But it's nice to have it confirmed. Now, get out of here, Drach. And you can tell your client that whoever sliced Liko Batom did her a favor. He was a lecher, a user of females, and involved with at least one Upper-Tier type."

"Selva Delrey?"

She said nothing, but her face told me I was right.

"Thanks, Guards Captain Atterson. You've confirmed what I suspected."

"Out!"

I let her have the last word.

I made my way through the halls to the plaza outside. Not even noon, and I had a lot to do before sundown. I glanced upwards, towards the looming scarp of Admin Hill. Did I want to attempt to interview the lads in their parent's aeries?? Not necessary, I decided. I had other, more pressing business.

Once again I headed out into the bright afternoon sunlight. I didn't look behind me as I crossed the plaza to the line of pedishaws. If someone was still following me, I wanted to be sure they could see where I was headed.

vi

Splurging on a pedishaw instead of using the carrier meant more coin, but it also meant I didn't have to climb halfway up the Striver's Hill, and the stretching and pummeling at the baths had worn off. I was feeling the sundew stings on my legs and arms, and the slash across my cheek was starting to burn.

I picked a driver in Pangkoti gear—loose trou tied at the ankle so they wouldn't catch in the wheel-chain, striped loose jacket worn over coarse cotton shirt, twist of cloth around the head, tucked under so it wouldn't flap in the rising breeze. I told him to wait for me and handed him some coin to make sure he did.

Then I knocked firmly on the gate.

A new face appeared; the previous gatekeeper must have been relieved of his post. Poor sod, he'd have a hard time finding work as a servant if he'd been chased out of the Vikk house for letting Betriz out of her prison.

I noted Kaisrin's red pedishaw in the courtyard. So, the clan was gathered. So much the better; I wouldn't have to repeat what I had to say, and it saved me the trouble of tracking her down.

I thought I saw the glint of a skimmer somewhere behind the house. Was Affrey back from his victory? Or did Teedo think he rated a skimmer? I wouldn't like to be a pedishaw driver, hauling someone the size of Teedo Vikk up and down Striver's Hill.

I followed the doorkeeper into the tiled entry foyer and started up the stairs. The tall servant in Pangkoti headgear stopped me.

"You may not go there."

"I want to speak with Junior Merchant Betriz Vikk," I stated.

"She is seeing no one." The servant stood firmly in the middle of the stair, daring me to shove him aside.

"Has a Medico been brought to attend her?" I was getting a very bad feeling about Betriz.

"She refuses all assistance."

"She's not seeing anyone!" Kaisrin Vikk called from the hallway. "You have to report to my mother. Please!"

I moved down the stairs and followed Kaisrin back to the little office from which Master Merchant Vikk ruled her shops and suppliers. It wasn't enough for her to take a percentage of the profit from each shop; she also had to be making a fair amount on the stock she bought in bulk from factories, packing mills, and even directly from the farms who supplied the factories and mills. Vikk-shops was a lot more than just a few small businesses; it was an empire.

She sat, as always, at a small table cluttered with papers, a short, plump female dressed in a rusty black gown that had furbelows and fringes not seen in Lorr for twenty years. A scrap of lace covered her white hair, scraped back into a practical knot at the base of her neck.

Teedo lurked behind her, trying to efface himself. Not easy to do, given his girth. Kaisrin took her place beside him. The two of them glanced at their mother, looking terrified of what she might say or do.

Elder Vikk ignored me for a bit while she scanned one of the many papers. Then she looked me over, marking my wounds, all incurred in her service.

"Where have you been? You were supposed to report to me as soon as you knew who was behind these attacks on my family."

"I wanted to repair my appearance," I said smoothly. "And I didn't want to accuse anyone without proof."

"Proof will be found," Elder Vikk said with a decided nod. "Who is it?"

"I'm not sure," I equivocated. "If I could speak with Junior Merchant Betriz, I would have a better idea of why she went to..." I hesitated.

"The establishment known as Smokey Joe's." Elder Vikk pronounced the name with a shudder of disgust. "A low tavern, frequented by disreputable persons."

Teedo shifted from foot to foot like a naughty scholar caught cheating on his examinations.

"It's not all that bad, Mam."

"It is one of the places you frequent with your hangers-on." His mother didn't even look at him. "And you dared to take you sister there!"

"Devon Delrey isn't low," Teedo protested "And going to Smokey Joe's was simply logical. We'd been through the shops in Fishmarket Sector, and we passed through the Waterfront on our way back to Striver's Hill. We ran into Selva coming from a run in her boat—"

"Selva Delrey?" I interrupted the flow of excuses. "On the Waterfront?"

"She's got a new boat," Teedo explained. "Quite fast, runs like the wind. She's become quite keen on the water since she's been seeing... ah..."

"Captain Ishka Kunine," I finished for him. "Whose ships are under attack, even as we speak."

"Captain Kunine is not under discussion," Elder Vikk declared. "And I do not approve of your friendship with

Selva Delrey. The creature is a disgrace to her clan. I have heard distressing rumors of her liaisons. She even had the effrontery to approach me with an offer of a union with Affrey. I told her I prefer none of my offspring deal with her except on the most formal basis. Affrey has better, more important things to do than dance attendance on a female of her reputation, no matter how much attention her entertainments bring. He does not need to parade himself before the populace. He is a hero! His father would be so proud of him!" She gazed at the portrait of the late Olber Vikk, hung on the wall where she could stare at it for inspiration.

"But, Mam," Kaisrin began. "We can't ignore her or refuse her invitations. She's Family."

"She may be your spouse's sibling, Kaisrin, but I would prefer you limit your contacts with her to mere politeness at family gatherings."

"It's not that easy, Mam. Devon likes her, and she does throw marvelous parties. You never know who you'll meet at one of them."

"Singers and artists, scribes of wretched stories, I suppose?" Elder Vikk dripped distaste.

"Singers like Liko Batom," I put in. "I heard him, just before his…accident."

They all stared at me. They had forgotten I was in the room.

"The singer who met his unfortunate end in Betriz's presence?" So, Elder Vikk had learned that much about what went down at Smokey's Joe's.

"The same. I think Junior Merchant Betriz was lured to the place by a note that implied he wanted to see more of her."

"And why would she want to see more of *him*?" Elder Vikk sneered.

"She was very taken with him," Teedo offered. "Selva had him over to our table when we went there, after our tour of the Fishmarket. Any friend of Selva's can't be all that bad."

"Oh, can't they?" More sarcasm from his mother sent Teedo back to his corner.

"I believe Junior Merchant Betriz was not completely herself during her stay at the, um, establishment," I said, trying to mollify the outraged elder. "The Dark Ones at the shrine where we took her seemed to think she'd been given a narcotic, possibly weed, so that she would remain quiet." I was the one who thought she'd been dosed, but the Dark Ones would back me up if necessary.

"To what end? No ransom was demanded, was it?" Elder Vikk looked to Kaisrin.

"If a notice came, I did not see it."

I took a deep breath. I didn't know how much Betriz had told anyone about her adventures into the darker side of town.

"It is possible that she was being held not for ransom, but for a more, um, intimate reason." I let it go at that. "And with an audience," I added, just to make the point.

Kaisrin let out a horrified gasp. "Selva wouldn't allow such a thing! Not with Betriz!"

Teedo turned red with embarrassment.

"I had no idea… Such things aren't done!"

Having set off the bomb, I tried to defuse the situation before someone had apoplexy.

"Whatever was planned did not occur. There was some confusion, a confrontation between some of the, um, more disreputable patrons and the City Guards, and I was able to get Junior Merchant Betriz out before any real damage was done to her person or her reputation." Unless the Delrey lad started another gossip chain, and he hadn't, as far as I knew.

"*Mpfh*," Elder Vikk grunted, and thought things over while Teedo and Kaisrin fidgeted.

I heard a sudden spatter of footsteps overhead, a slamming door.

"If I may be allowed to speak with Junior Merchant Betriz?" I tried again.

"I cannot allow—" Elder Vikk was interrupted when a servant burst into the room.

"Mam! It's Junior Merchant Betriz! "

"What's she done?"

Teedo stared out the window into the courtyard. "She's taken Kaisrin's pedishaw!"

"And my driver?" Kaisrin joined Teedo at the window.

"Shoved him aside!" Teedo stared in amazement. "Founder's faith, she's mounted the wheel-seat herself!"

"Where can she be going?" Mam Vikk wondered.

"I didn't know she could ride!" Teedo exclaimed.

"She must have been practicing for something like this," Kaisrin moaned.

"Close the gate!" Elder Vikk ordered. "Send for the Guard at once. She must be stopped!"

"Too late for that," I said. "I'll get her!" I didn't bother with polite niceties. I ran through the hall, out the front door, into the courtyard, where the Delrey driver was protesting the theft of his vehicle and my driver was gawking at the red pedishaw rapidly rolling down the hill

"After her!" I yelled, heaving myself onto the back seat as my driver got his wheels turning.

And the race was on!

vii

Betriz wasn't an expert on wheels, but a pedishaw isn't all that hard to maneuver, not like the two-wheelers used by most of the tech-mechs for personal transport. She bounced along, veering down Striver's Hill, wobbling between the high walls surrounding the other mansion while I yelled at her to stop.

My driver, more skilled, maneuvered his wheels so we quickly pulled up alongside her. I leaned across the gap and shouted, "This is no go, Betriz! You can't run away from what you've started!"

"I won't go back!" She let gravity take over and sped down the hill. "Liko is waiting for me!"

"Liko is dead!" I yelled at her.

"I don't believe you! I got a note from him…"

We'd reached the bottom of the hill, where the carrier stops to let folks off. One had just pulled in, and people were stepping down. The Guardsman on duty popped out of the guardhouse and waved madly for us to stop.

My driver slowed down to avoid hitting pedestrians, but Betriz shot between the guardhouse and the waiting-station and careened into the kiosk, sending mags flying. The vendor screamed at her in Lorran, Pangkoti, and some other dialect I couldn't place.

Betriz didn't stop, but zoomed toward Grand Boulevard, skirts flying high, revealing her full-bottom drawers. The Guardsman took a minute to stare, then yelled something while he fumbled under his jacket for his whistle. He blew a warning toot.

Betriz ignored him and turned onto the Grand Boulevard, right in front of another bunch of carrier passengers. The seat of the pedishaw whacked the side of the carrier, but other than that, no damage done. The passengers gawked, the Transporteer squawked, and behind us the City Guard ducked into his little shack to report a runaway pedishaw on his comm.

"Keep going!" I ordered.

My driver bent over the handlebars and showed what he was made of. I read the name on the tag fastened to the seat.

"Aziz! A silver if you catch her!"

He used his strong legs to push forward, dodging walkers and wheels.

Betriz had picked the worst possible time for her escape—just before sundown, the hour of the Promenade, when the Upper Tier displayed their finery by tooling their pedishaws and wheels up and down the Grand Boulevard on either side of the carrier tracks so that everyone who isn't Upper Tier can admire them.

However, Betriz was going east towards the river, following the walkers, while everyone else on wheels was heading west away from it. Bit by bit, we gained on her, while some of the flashier Uppers shouted encouragement and the Lowers cursed at the disturbance.

Between obstruction caused by the walkers and the effort of pedaling, Betriz slowed down, losing some of the enthusiasm that had propelled her into this wild dash for freedom. Aziz bent over his handlebars, dodging another carrier and working around handcarts loaded with goods for the markets around the Central Plaza.

"We've nearly got her!" I crowed. "Push on, Friend Driver, and you'll get extra silver when we nab her!"

"She's headed for the bridge!" Aziz panted. "I cannot go over the bridge, Friend Passenger. It is forbidden for Lorr pedishaws to transport passengers into Flatlands."

"Death and Destruction!" I cursed. "Can you get to her before she reaches the bridge?"

"I can try…" He put on one final desperate burst of speed.

Betriz's pedishaw wobbled and stopped. She hopped off, clearly winded, and clung to the News Posts on the Lorr side of the bridge. Then, she staggered forward, towards the wharves where the pleasure-boats were tied up.

I had my coin ready. I slid two silvers into Aziz's hand as I leapt off the back of the pedishaw and ran madly, shoving walkers, cyclers, and handcarts out of my way. I reached out to grab her by the sleeve…

Something hit me in the back of the head…and that was all I knew for a while.

viii

I woke up with an ache in the back of my head and a sinking feeling in the pit of my stomach. It was just as well I hadn't had much more than a cup of chai and a sweet cracker at the baths, or I would have left the remains on the front of my jacket.

I was lying on my side on some kind of shelf that went up and down and side to side. My legs were tied at the ankles, my hands tied behind my back. I tried to squirm into a sitting position, banged my head on the shelf above me, flipped over and wound up on the floor. No, it was a deck. I must be on a boat.

My last gift from Ficus hadn't worn off yet. I could smell the river, feel the surge of water close by, hear the *glug-glug* of water and the *slap-slap* of waves hitting a hard surface.

I assessed my surroundings as my vision cleared. I was in some kind of room—a cabin, with windows that let in enough light to see by, not below the waterline but more or less even with it.

Whose boat was it? I had no problems with anyone on the Waterfront; my father's reputation protected me from most hassles. The only one who might wish me ill was Selva Delrey. Selva had taken to boating. Ergo, I must be on Selva Delrey's boat.

I tried to recall how I'd gotten here, but the last thing I remembered was seeing Betriz hanging onto one of the stanchions at the bridge-head, and someone coming

192

to greet her. Then, a sharp pain at the back of my head, and two arms around my shoulders, and… nothing.

Until I opened my eyes in this cabin.

"So, you're awake." A silky-smooth voice, with an Upper-Tier accent.

"Selva Delrey. How's business?"

I hitched myself over to the bulkhead, wiggled around, and managed to get into a sitting position so I could face her.

She'd taken care to dress in what she probably thought was Pirate Mode, starting with lizard-skin boots, dyed black, with impossibly high narrow heels and pointed toes. Tight black silk trou, leather jacket open to show a loose shirt, also open to reveal a lot of chest and several gold chains. Black hair twisted into many tight braids, each one tipped with a gold bead. Facepaint dead white, with red lips and black circles around the eyes. Very dramatic, totally lost on me.

I was more interested in her associates. Two hardbodies stood just behind her—I'd seen them in Smokey Joe's —and Betriz Vikk hovered in the background, nervously clutching a shooter, as if the thing would go off in her hand before she was ready to fire it.

"Nice to see you, Betriz," I greeted her. "I see you made it to your meeting place. A pity Liko won't be here. He's in the Dark Ones' temple, awaiting examination."

"He can't be!" Betriz squeaked. "Selva said…She told me…"

"A pack of lies," I snapped just before Selva slapped me across the face, aiming directly for the sundew burn.

"Quiet!" she ordered. She didn't even look at the hardbodies. "Brutus, Casak, tell the pilot to cast off."

One of the hardbodies asked, "Now? We're not loaded yet."

"Better go while you can," I said. "I expect company at any moment. Betriz isn't the most skillful pedishaw
driver in the world, and I had a few followers this morning while I was making my rounds. Want to take odds
on who gets here first, Fatsos or Guards?"

"We'll be down the river by the time they get here,"
Selva boasted. "As for Liko—that was too bad, but he had
a loose tongue. It was only a matter of time until he was
stopped."

"No!" Betriz squealed. "You told me…I was going
to…We would be…" She started to sniffle.

"Oh, shut up, you silly fool!"

Betriz gasped as if *she'd* been struck. She'd probably
never heard such language, certainly not addressed to her.

"What's wrong, Selva?" I didn't bother with polite
honorifics. "It's only right that Betriz should know what
she's getting into. Or didn't you bother to tell her you'd
arranged for her little adventure to be witnessed by half of
the Admin Academy? They were even selling tickets!"

Selva's smirk told me everything I wanted to know. "I
wasn't there, and you can't prove I knew anything about
that incident."

"Your baby brother told his classmates about the 'special presentation'," I guessed. "How would he know, if
you didn't tell him? It's not the sort of thing Admin lads
find out about, not unless they have a contact at the Waterfront."

Betriz stepped closer to Selva. "It's not true, is it? Why is she saying these things? Where is Liko? You promised I'd be with Liko…"

I had tested the bonds while I was wriggling. Now I started twisting my wrists back and forth, feeling a slight give. Whoever had tied the knots hadn't done a very good job.

All I had to do was keep Selva's attention away from finishing me off.

"Liko's dead," I told Betriz, the most brutally honest way I could. "The hardbody who got him in the back hit something inside, and we must have made it worse while we were trying to get him out of Smokey Joe's. They tried, but even the Dark Ones and their special boffins couldn't save him."

"But…Selva said…"

"Selva's lying to you," I told her again. "She's been planning this for a long time. Haven't you, Banker Delrey? Or perhaps I should call you, Captain-Banker? Assassin-Banker?"

"I don't know what you mean!" Selva sneered.

"Sure you do." I twisted my hands, ignoring the pain in my wrists as the ropes bit into the flesh. "You set it all up. Getting Teedo interested in Marla Lily, making the bad coin and bringing it in, forcing the Vikk-shops to stock bad merch."

"That wasn't my idea, that was Ishka's," Selva objected. "I am not a Merchant, I have no interest in clet."

"But you convinced Betriz to order it," I said. "She'd never have done it on her own."

"I could have!" Betriz found her voice at last. "And it *was* a good idea, to buy a shipload of the clet, only how was I to know it wouldn't sell? Fishmarket folk are Transporteers and pedishaw drivers, housecleaners and day servants."

"But they know good clet from bad, and they won't buy bad merch." I felt liquid on my wrist. Maybe I'd drawn blood? I braced myself against the bulkhead, ignoring the rasp of the fibers against my skin.

I strained to hear what was happening outside. I heard waves lapping. I smelled the rank weedy odor of the river. Overhead, there were footsteps stamping, someone shouting. The boat was bobbing up and down, but not moving forward.

The only question was—Which side of the river were we on? Because my carefully laid plans wouldn't work if Selva's boat was moored on the Flatlands side, where the City Guards had no authority and the Fatsos fought the Flatlanders on a regular schedule.

"What I don't understand, Selva, is why? Why go to all this trouble, just to make the Vikk clan look bad? Bringing one of Fee M'Farr's popsies into their house, informing Admin that they're running bad merch and bad coin, and then this matter of shaming Betrriz? It makes no sense. There's no profit in it."

"Is that all you can think of, Pola Drach? Profit?" Selva snarled. "I should have expected it. You're nothing but Second Ship at heart. You have no idea of anything besides profit and loss, coin and collecting it. You don't understand honor. You can't understand what it means to see your family shamed, destroyed, by upstarts like the

Vikks, who are only Merchants—Second Ship Merchants. Olber Vikk was a mere shopowner when he borrowed from my father."

"And paid him back," Betriz retorted. "Banker Gregor Delrey was paid in full. Papa always told us to pay our debts, and the Vikks always do." At least she had enough gumption in her to defend her family.

"Paid in full?" Selva spat out. "Oh, yes, the original sum was paid, but once that was done, there was nothing else! All those shops, bought with the proceeds from the first, those should have been part of the contract."

"Should have been isn't was," I corrected her. "And all that happened nearly thirty years ago, when you were in your Mother's Guild care. Why bring it up now?"

"Devon's stipend," Betriz said suddenly. "He asked to have his stipend from the Vikk-shops increased."

"How do you know?" I asked.

"I saw the letter he sent to Mam," Betriz said, as light dawned behind that dull façade. "He wanted more money. Mam disapproved."

"So he could invest in an airship." I recalled Kaisrin telling me about it when she'd asked me to find out where Devon was getting extra coin.

"Which Mam refused to do," Betriz said. She stared at Selva. "Is that why you asked me to come to your soirée? To get Devon's stipend increased?"

"More likely to wedge herself into the Vikk money-pile," I said. "You may not want to dirty your own hands with buying and selling, but you like coin, Selva Delrey. You like coin, but you love power more. You're drawn to it.

"And banking's not where the power lies these days, it's the Merchant's Guild controls Lorr. It's why you went after Affrey Vikk, and it's why you've hooked up with Ishka Kunine."

I felt the ropes give way just enough so I could slide one hand out of the bindings, It hurt, but I could bear it. Now, if I could keep Selva's interest on me long enough for one of the two sets of watchers to figure out where I was...

She glared at me, but didn't move. "You have a nasty mouth on you, Pola Drach. I should have had you silenced long ago, when you were in the Guards."

"You couldn't do it then, and you can't do it now. Should have gagged me while you had the chance, Selva. Try it now, and you'll get your hand bitten."

She took a step closer. "You know nothing!"

"True, but I can guess. My guess is that you approached Mam Vikk with the idea of finishing the Vikk-Delrey connection by uniting yourself with Teedo, only she'd have none of it, and neither would he.

"So, you tried the other way, getting Affrey interested, but he's no fool and saw through you. Then you introduced Teedo to Marla Lily, who was supposed to be one of your 'discoveries'. Clearly, you didn't know she was Fee M'Farr's popsy. Or that she was carrying his offspring."

Selva blanched, then flushed. "I did not! She was supposed to attract Teedo, and lead him into a disastrous union. I didn't plan on the servant removing her."

"But he did, and I came on the scene. And I've been wondering just what Marla Lily was supposed to do, once she got in with the Vikks, considering she was a lot more to M'Farr than just a popsy. She was one of M'Farr's top females, an Assassin, only *acting* as a Clothier's Model.

"Who was she supposed to remove, Selva? Teedo? Or maybe Mam Vikk herself? And then, Selva, who would take over the Vikk-shops? Teedo? Not likely. Affrey? Off on Aerial Corps heroics. Kaisrin? With Devon's help… and Betriz's. She's been right at the heart of the Vikk-shops since she was old enough to do the addition on the books."

Selva grew redder under the white paint, her face tightening with every word. Betriz edged farther and farther away from her.

"You've been worked, Betriz," I jeered. "Selva's been working you from the start. She invited you to a party, made much of you, got you to order the clet, and then laid an information against you with Admin. They've been investigating the bad coin and how it's being passed through the Vikk-shops. When the ax falls, it'll fall on you, Junior Merchant Betriz Vikk, not on Banker Selva Delrey. She'll be far away, laughing at you with her own popsy, Captain Iska Kunine."

"You don't like Mam!" Betriz sputtered at Selva. "You called her a miserable stingy old woman! You're always telling me how much better I would be at running the Vikk-shops than Teedo or Kaisrin."

"And she made sure you were introduced to Liko Batom, even though she knows your Mam doesn't think much of entertainers," I added. "And who was it who told you he was waiting for you at Smokey Joe's the night you left the mansion?"

"It was you!" Betriz gasped. "Selva, *you* sent me the note. I thought it was one of the Delrey runners who brought it, but he was in the shadows, so I couldn't be sure."

"That's Selva's way," I said, egging Betriz on. "She doesn't do the deed herself. Oh, no, a Delrey doesn't get her hands dirty. She gets someone else to do it for her. She puts Marla Lily in Teedo's way, she convinces Ishka Kunine to bring his ship to Lorr, she gets her brother to bring his Admin pals to watch you get done by some hardbody you don't even know…all because she's been slighted by someone she feels is her inferior. You're pathetic, Selva Delrey!"

"You little…" She stepped forward again, but not quite close enough for me to reach.

"I'm surprised you took the personal trouble to go to my rooms," I went on. "Taking your vengeance on Ficus! Stomping a helpless plant!"

"You can't know…"

"You shouldn't wear those boots. Lizard skin drops scales, and there will be little bits of Ficus left on the soles. And maybe I'll let the Admin boffins match the marks on my floor with those ridiculous dagger-heels of yours. Probably the only time you ever did anything for yourself, and for what? To make me unhappy?"

She took one more step…and I wrenched my hands out of the loosened bonds. My feet were still tied at the ankles, but I could swing my legs to knock her off those high heels. She fell forward, right on top of me.

I rolled her off me, and we grappled on the heaving deck, scratching and screeching like a couple of feuding

Licensees while overhead there was confused stamping and shouting.

I grabbed a hank of hair, and the twisted braids came off, revealing a close-cut graying bob.

"Shoot her! Shoot her!" Selva gasped as she struggled in my grip

Betriz hovered somewhere above us as we rolled around on the deck. Selva clawed at my face, while I tried to kick my feet loose. Betriz shrieked and dropped the shooter. It went off, sending something over our heads into the woodwork.

And then hands were pulling me off Selva, and Sara Atterson's clipped tones announced, "In the name of the City Guards of Lorr, I arrest you, Selva Delrey, on the charge of passing false coin!"

I wobbled to my feet. "How's business, Captain Atterson? What kept you?"

ix

Selva scrambled to her feet, and screamed something vile as she attacked Atterson. Atterson neatly sidestepped her, used one of the moves we studied in Training, and nearly brought Selva down, but Selva was ready for that one and headed for the cabin door. Two guardsmen grabbed her as she tried to get out the door. She kicked, screamed, clawed, and yelled for her hardbodies, but they were already in custody. One more guardsman held Betriz.

"Betriz Vikk!" one of the guards announced. "You are charged with taking a vehicle from its owner, disturbing the peace of Lorr by dangerous driving, and possession of an illegal weapon. Do you understand the charges?"

Betriz looked wildly about, seeking aid, advice, comfort, and not finding any.

"The vehicle in question belongs to her sister, and the weapon is Selva's," I put in. "But she definitely drove that pedishaw on the public roads in a dangerous manner. Plenty of witnesses, too. Better confess, Betriz, and let your mam deal with the fines."

"As for you!" Atterson glared at me. "What sort of game were you playing, Drach? Leading my people on a wild beast chase across Lorr?"

"I knew you'd have someone on my trail," I said. "You should have Fee M'Farr train your people. It took me at least three minutes to spot his tracker. I knew yours was there as soon as I got into Aziz's pedishaw."

"I'll look into it." Atterson "You know, Drach, you look terrible."

"I've seen better days," I admitted. "You don't happen to have a Dark Medico with you, do you?"

"Not here, but I'm sure we can accommodate you at Admin." Atterson yelled to someone outside the cabin. "Take these three on the skimmer! And search this vessel for contraband!"

The guard hauled me out of the cabin onto the deck, and I could see where I was by the light of the electrics on the Waterfront. The sun was down, the Gold Moon was just up.

Selva's boat was a refitted fishing smack, tricked out with fancy paint and shiny brass. The crew were herded into one corner of the deck, all protesting in Pangkoti they were only hired hands, nothing to do with either Selva Delrey or Ishka Kunine.

"We found this person below." A guard hauled a skinny male specimen forward. "I can't understand his lingo, but I think he's some kind of tech. He's got a lot of metal down there, pressed into circles."

He handed one to Atterson, who handled it with two fingers, very carefully.

"This looks a lot like a silver coin," she said. "But there's no denomination or sigil on it."

"That's because it goes blank if you touch it," I told her. "I'm willing to bet a good silver that you'll find some kind of apparatus that imprints Lorr sigils and denominations on it, just long enough for it to be passed from one hand to another, before it goes blank again. Clever, these Pangkoti!"

Atterson smirked at Selva. "Stupid of you to keep the makings and the tech on your own boat. I suppose Captain Kunine expected you to pick him up when he sailed back into Lorr at the head of a triumphant fleet. Sorry to tell you this, Banker Delrey, but the last anyone saw of Captain Kunine, he was headed south to whatever waits for him in Pangkot. Or maybe he'll skip the ceremonies, and go straight for the Southern Continent, where he can start a settlement of his own. In either case, he won't be coming back for you."

Selva's expression flickered, just for a moment. Then her jaw tightened, her lips thinned, and she looked past everyone.

"You cannot do this to me. I am Banker Selva Delrey!"

"Right now, you are a prisoner of the Administration of New Earth," Atterson declared. "Junior Merchant Vikk, you will accompany me to Administration to face charges. You may inform your family, so they can pay your fines.

"As for you, Independent Eye Pola Drach, you'd best come with us. There's a Medico at Admin who can take care of those scrapes and scratches, and you can report to Admin in full."

A crowd had gathered on the docks, ready to comment on the spectacle of one of Lorr's most prominent females being marched down the pier to the waiting official skimmer. There would be Post Six notices describing Selva's demeanor, her clothing, all the charges against her, along with plenty of innuendo and speculation about her relationship with Captain Ishka Kunine.

Betriz got a different response. A bunch of juvenile males yelled when she made her appearance on the docks. Her wild ride across Lorr was hailed as a feat of daring, an escape from the tyranny of a cruel parent. Sympathetic whispers followed her as she was shoved into the official skimmer. There were even a few cheers from the younger pedishaw drivers, who admired her exploit.

As for me? I hid behind the largest guardsmen, slid into the last seat in the skimmer, and held on tight as it lifted off. I don't really like skimmers, even though they're the fastest way of getting from here to there. I'm never sure when the electric that moves them is going to give out, or whether the fans under the chassis are really strong enough to keep the thing in the air.

The procession wound up at Admin Hill, where Captain Atterson was greeted by a mixed lot of guards and civilians who closed in around Selva and Betriz. I was herded away into the stark interior of the building, that complex of tunnels carved into the hills that surround Lorr.

I was put into the hands of Dark Ones Medicos, who bound my wounds, dosed me with antibios, and told me to rest. I was grateful for the bandages, allowed the Med-tech to spray me with whatever would keep infection away, and was placed into a cubicle with a hard cot and nothing else.

I asked the female med-tech to send someone to my digs for a clean outfit. Then I gave in to the sedative for a few hours.

I woke with a desperate need for the elimination place, and the feeling that I'd missed something important. The Med-tech hurried into the cubicle, accompanied by a male City Guard carrying a set of trou and jacket that didn't belong to me.

"Get dressed," he ordered. "You're summoned to give evidence."

I shucked my soiled clothes, dressed in the ill-fitting garments provided for me, and followed the guard down one hall and around another, all brilliantly lit with electrics. No expense spared for Admin!

Of course, there were no windows.

I had no idea how much time had elapsed between the arrest and this examination. I judged it to be hours, not days. I joined the crowd in the examination room as the guard bawled out, "All rise for Legal Examination, Magistrate Turgo Maras presiding!"

The Magistrate, Turgo Maras, was a dark-complexioned male, broad-shouldered and bald-headed, draped in the traditional black robe. I'd given evidence before him a few times when my clients decided to bring their grievances before Admin. He was a strict interpreter of the Regulations of Lorr, the rules laid down by the Founders and expanded by generations of Lorrans over the generations since the First Landing.

The interval between the arrest and the examination had been long enough for the various parties concerned to gather their legal minions. All were present in the small examination room, and all were yelling loudly for attention.

Loudest and most numerous was the Vikk contingent—Teedo Vikk in full cry, tall and stout with voice booming and blustering, accompanied by not one but two advocates. One was for the Vikk clan personally, the other a Merchant's Guild rep, both in standard Merchant gear of matching gray jacket and trou.

Devon Delrey had taken a place as far away from Teedo as he could, with a Banker's Guild advocate hovering between him and Selva. Selva had managed to put herself into some kind of order. She'd got fresh clothing but hadn't been able to renew her facepaint. She looked haggard and worn in a gray set of jacket and trou, her braids replaced by a more sedate wig over her close-cropped graying hair.

Caught between the Delreys and the Vikks was Kaisrin, not knowing which family to support—the one she was born into or the one she was bound to. My money was on Vikk, not Delrey, but genes don't always trump coin.

Behind the Upper Tier were the two hardbodies from the boat, represented by Ratty from the Assassins's Guild.

My driver, Aziz, was behind them, at the very back of the room, and a squad of guards kept curious onlookers outside the doors. Captain Atterson consulted with the Admin drones seated at the table in front of the dais where the Magistrate had his bench, the official desk commanding a view of the room. The uniformed bailiff, a harried-looking female of middle years, was trying to make some sense of this rabble.

"All rise and greet the Honorable Turgo Maras!" she bawled for a second time over the babble of voices.

There was a brief silence while Magistrate Maras took his place. Then the uproar started again.

"I demand to know why my sibling has been placed under guard!" Teedo roared.

"My sibling has done nothing wrong!" Devon whined.

"The Honorable Guild of Forgers, Assassins, Thieves, and Swindlers had nothing to do with this!" That was Ratty.

"Quiet!" Magistrate Maras boomed. There was silence. "That's better," he said. "Now we can proceed like rational beings. This is not a trial, but an examination of the facts, to determine if a crime has been committed, as defined by the Regulations of Lorr. Is that understood?"

He glared at the assemblage, then turned to Atterson. "Captain Atterson, you have brought these persons here. Explain the charges."

She took a deep breath. "There are several charges, Your Honor. To begin with, Junior Merchant Betriz Vikk is accused of taking a vehicle—to wit, a pedishaw—belonging to her sibling Merchant-Banker Kaisrin Vikk-Delrey without permission, and driving it in a dangerous and reckless manner through the public roads, causing great consternation, destroying property, and making herself a spectacle for ridicule, thus damaging the Vikk family reputation." She handed the Magistrate a paper, presumably the official report of Betriz's wild dash for freedom.

"Quite a complaint," Maras commented, checking over the report. "Is Junior Merchant Betriz Vikk present?" He scanned the people arrayed before him.

Betriz stepped forward. "That's me."

"Is this report accurate?" Maras asked.

"What do you mean?" Betriz quavered.

"Did you, indeed, steal a pedishaw?"

"I took it, but I didn't steal it…I just borrowed it. I was going to give it back…"

"And did you ride through the public thoroughfare on said vehicle in a dangerous manner?"

"You can't go all that fast on a pedishaw!" Teedo burst out.

"And you are…?"

"You know who I am, Turgo Maras. I've seen you at the Guild Hall many a time. I am Merchant Teedo Vikk, here to defend the interest of Clan Vikk from the offensive tactics of Administration hacks—"

"Spare me the political rant, Merchant Vikk. Are there witnesses to this theft and subsequent destructive action by Junior Merchant Betriz Vikk?"

Aziz bounded forward. "I was there, I saw all!"

"And you are…?" Maras looked over the report.

"I am Aziz, I am a Transport Guild member in good standing, I pay my Guild fee every month, I am a strong driver, I work hard."

"I don't doubt it."

"Transporteer Aziz was driving the pedishaw that followed Junior Merchant Vikk across Lorr," Atterson explained.

"And why was he following her?"

"That was my fault." I edged through the crowd to the front of the room. "I am Independent Eye…"

"Pola Drach," Maras said with a sigh. "Your name also appears on this report."

"Yes, Your Honor. I observed Junior Merchant Vikk leaving the Vikk residence on Striver's Hill and tried to stop her, but she kept going."

"A very bad diver," Aziz put in. "She hit the public carrier, and upset two handcarts. I did not touch any other vehicle, I am a good driver!"

"I'm sure you are." Maras looked at the paper again. "According to this report, the stolen pedishaw was abandoned at the entrance to the crossing bridge that leads to Flatlands. Is that true?"

"Yes, but I was going to give it back to Kaisrin as soon as I could," Betriz protested.

"So, you stole—"

"I didn't steal it, I *borrowed* it!" Betriz wouldn't give up on that point.

"Merchant-Banker Vikk-Delrey, did you give permission for Junior Merchant Vikk to use the vehicle in question?" The magistrate was sticking to the Regs.

"I would have allowed her to use it if she had asked, but she didn't ask." Kaisrin turned to Betriz. "Why didn't you ask, Betriz? I would have taken you where you wanted to go."

"No, you wouldn't. Mam wouldn't allow it!" Betriz faced her sister, her face contorted in fury. "All of you, you wouldn't let me leave! I was a prisoner in that house! I had to get out!"

"Removed vehicle without permission." Maras made a note on the report. "That, according to the Regulations of Lorr, is theft. You may face trial, or pay the requisite fines."

The Vikk advocates immediately converged on the Magistrate, who smacked his gavel and waved them off.

"Captain Atterson, continue, if you please. Why are the rest of these persons here?"

"The Guards were summoned to the Waterfront to answer a report of assault and battery, followed by forcible removal of the person of Pola Drach to a vessel owned by Banker Selva Delrey."

"Really?" Maras turned his gaze to Selva and her cohorts.

Aziz sprang up again, eager to again claim a place in the unfolding drama. "I saw it all! Those two..." He indicated the Fatso hardbodies. "They were at the bridge.

One takes this female person by the arm, the other hit my passenger on the head with a little stick. I see them drag her her to the boat, I go to the guards, I tell them what I see, they call for help."

"Which I assume was forthcoming," Maras said. "Is there an advocate for the Assassin's Guild present?"

Ratty stood up

"Another familiar face. What have you to say, Assassin Ratisov?"

Ratty prepared to defend his guild's latest recruits. "These two males, Brutus and Casak, are recent refugees from Pangkot. They are employed by the Delrey Bank as general bodyguards, protecting Delrey property. They were placed on the boat belonging to Banker Selva Delrey by her sibling, Banker Devon Delrey, to protect Delrey property. They have no connection with anything else."

"We didn't know nothing," Casak, the shorter of the two, repeated in heavily accented Lorran.

"And we still don't." That was Brutus, the big fellow.

"That's the one who was supposed to do the evil deed on Betriz!" I accused, pointing at him.

Magistrate Maras looked at the paper before him, then at me. "There's nothing here about an assault on Junior Merchant Vikk."

"Because it didn't happen," I explained. "But this character was hired to…" I stumbled on the words.

"Hey, it was supposed to be a reward for good service, giving me a juicy little thing to play with," Brutus protested. "But now that I see her in daylight, she's no girl, she's an old bag of bones, not worth my time."

I didn't know whether to be appalled by his callous description or sorry for Betriz, dismissed as not even fit for a rapist's attention. Teedo roared something about scoundrels, Brutus surged at him, and it took four guards, one pair on each, to separate them.

Maras whacked his gavel to call for order. "Captain Atterson, continue your report. Why did you board the vessel?"

"When we approached the boat, we heard sounds of a fight." Atterson stated. "I ordered the guards aboard—"

"Without warrant or permission!" Selva finally got to speak for herself.

"None needed, under the circumstance," Atterson retorted. "We found Independent Eye Pola Drach and Banker Selva Delrey in the cabin…"

"That wretched woman assaulted me!" Selva yelled.

"Moderate your language!" Maras warned her. "There will be no obscenity used in this examination room!" He turned to me. "Independent Eye Drach, did you assault Banker Delrey?"

"Considering I was bound hand and foot, I think she's the one who did the assaulting," I said. "She slapped me, then ordered Junior Merchant Vikk to shoot me. I just tried to stop her leaving port."

"When we found them, Independent Eye Drach's ankles were tied together with twine," Atterson confirmed. "And if you read the Medico's report, there are marks on her hands and wrists consistent with having been similarly bound."

Maras made another note on his papers. "Very well. Banker Selva Delrey, what have you to say in your defense?"

"It's all a pack of nonsense," Selva said with a sneer. "I am one of the Banker Delreys, I don't have to give an account of my actions to anyone."

"One more thing," Atterson said before Maras could start his standard speech about the sanctity of Regulations, how the Founders drew them up when they landed twenty generation ago, how they guaranteed to all citizens of Lorr certain rights and obligations, and so on.

"During our occupation of the vessel, we discovered a cache of coins made of a certain alloy, not known to Lorr, with other evidence that leads us to suspect they are being used to disrupt the trade of Lorr. We also took a male into custody, said male being a native of Pangkot. conversant with the minting and engraving of coins."

"Counterfeit!" Ratty burst out. "Unsanctioned by the Honorable Guild of Forgers, Assassins, Thieves, and Swindlers!"

"And where is this person?" Maras scanned the room.

"He is being held by Admin Security." Atterson stated. "As he is a citizen of Pangkot, the Lorr Guilds have no jurisdiction over him, but the General Administration most certainly does. Our boffins are very interested in the metal alloy used in the making of the coins."

"*You* brought him in!" Ratty advanced on Selva. "He was found on your boat! You're bringing bad coin into Lorr, Banker Selva Delrey, unsanctioned by the Guild!"

"A very serious accusation, Banker Delrey. What have you to say to that?" Maras stared stonily at Selva.

Devon edged away from her. Selva said nothing.

"I see." Maras's voice was icy. "You prefer to remain silent. That is your right, under the Regulations."

"Death to the Regulations!" Selva burst out. "They mean nothing! They were laid out at another time, by people who wanted to organize, regulate everything! Regulations have no place on New Earth! Freedom for all!"

I'd had enough of Selva and her so-called freedom of action.

"Is that what Ishka Kunine's been feeding you? Don't be fooled. He's not out for anyone's freedom but his own. He's playing you, Selva, just like you're playing Betriz."

"He's on his way—" Selva shot back.

"As far as I know," the magistrate informed her, "Captain Ishka Kunine and his invasion fleet were turned back. He is headed towards the South Continent. Do not expect him to rescue you from your folly, Banker Delrey." He whacked the gavel. "Merchant Vikk, can you stand surety for your sibling?"

"I can authorize any payment of fines for damaged property," Teedo announced after a quick chat with Kaisrin. "The pedishaw in question is family property, and Merchant-Banker Kaisrin Vikk-Delrey is willing to forgo any accusations of theft or punishment appertaining thereto. If there is any further difficulty, send the appropriate documents to our offices at the Merchants' Guild Hall."

"It that case, Junior Merchant Betriz Vikk is remanded into the custody of her family until further notice."

Smack! went the gavel.

Devon leaped to his feet. "Magistrate, the Delrey Bank is willing to stand surety for Banker Selva Delrey."

Maras's gavel went down again. "The charges against Banker Selva Delrey are far more serious than mere theft. The coins in question will need careful examination by trained experts. There are also accusations of treasonable relations with an enemy of Lorr. Until the matters are resolved, Banker Selva Delrey will remain in the custody of the Administration of New Earth. That is all!"

"What about them?" Atterson indicated the two Pankoti.

"Hey, we were under orders!" the one named Brutus protested. "We're hired help. Assassins Guild, see?" He produced his badge and waved it proudly aloft.

Selva dismissed them with a sneer. "Not even worth the coin I spent on you. You couldn't even tie a prisoner securely."

"They will be disciplined by their Guildmaster, Fee M'Farr," Maras decreed. "This session is adjourned!" He stalked out, followed by the guards and their prisoner.

I had decided not to bring up the invasion of my digs. No one would pay for the damage to a single plant, anyway, not even a rare specimen like Ficus.

The examination room slowly cleared, as the various groups left for their respective vehicles. The Vikks shoved Betriz into the now-battered red pedishaw, while Teedo balanced on his tri-wheel and the two advocates took a less elaborate pedishaw. The Delrey contingent had a skimmer, as befit the leader of the Banker's Guild. Not the most recent model, but shiny and sleek, and faster than a pedishaw.

Kaisrin stood between the Vikks and the Delreys…and made her choice. She got into the pedishaw next to Betriz. Blood ties won over legal bonds, and Kaisrin would stay with her sister, not her husband.

Ratty and the two would-be Assassins were met by another black-coated squad, and the lot of them marched down the hill to the Assassins Guild House to face the wrath of Fee M'Farr. I suspected they would find themselves stranded on the outskirts of Flatlands, standing guard over the factories, swatting insects, and wishing they had never left Pangkot.

I was left alone in the plaza in front of Admin with Aziz.

"I should thank you," I told him, fumbling for coin in my pouch.

"I have already been paid," Aziz said with a grin. "And after this adventure is known, I will get many free meals and drinks when I tell how I saved the Independent Eye from assassins. All I ask is that when you need a pedishaw, you come to me. I am usually found at the stand near the Entertainers' Guild Hall."

"Enjoy the meals," I said, mounting the pedishaw. "Take me back to Fletcher's Food Shop—I think I've earned a day of rest."

xi

As always, there were consequences. Nothing happens in Lorr without discussion, rumor, and payment.

I gave the Vikk clan a day to consolidate, then presented myself at the mansion. It was Kaisrin, not Betriz, who led me to Master Merchant Drina Vikk this time. I handed my account to Elder Vikk, who handed it to Kaisrin.

"Pay it." Just that. No haggling, no questioning, not even a glance at the bottom figure.

Kaisrin counted out coins. I checked each one, rubbing it carefully just in case one of Selva's funny ones had slipped into the Vikk coffers.

"Remove yourself," Elder Vikk ordered. "Do not return."

"I sincerely hope I don't have to," I said, and I meant it. I hadn't wanted to get involved with the Vikk clan to begin with.

Kaisrin followed me to the door.

"I want to thank you for what you did for Betriz," she said, softly, so the hovering servants wouldn't hear.

"How's she doing?"

"The Medico says she's got some superficial scratches, but the sundew poison has been neutralized. She refuses to speak with anyone except her servant, and that only when necessary. Mam is quite put out with her. It is all very difficult." Kaisrin sighed.

"She'll get through it," I consoled her. "You Vikks are tougher than you look. Affrey should be home from the wars soon. Let him talk her out of the sulks."

Kaisrin's face brightened. "Affrey always got on better with Betriz than I do."

"And he's a war hero," I reminded her. "There should be a few celebrations in his honor. Maybe he'll escort her to some of them, get her away from this house, let her meet some people. Not the sort she'd meet at places like Smokey Joe's," I added.

"Mam won't like that." She glanced over her shoulder, as if her formidable mother were lurking behind her, listening to every word. "She expected Betriz to continue as her private secretary forever."

"Betriz has other ideas," I said. "I'll leave her to you, Merchant-Banker Vikk-Delrey."

"Only Merchant Vikk," Kaisrin said. "I do not wish to be associated with Banker Delrey. We may not dissolve our union, but I will not live in the same residence with the person who arranged to shame my family."

"I thought Selva was in Admin custody."

"She has been released." Kaisrin's sour expression told me what she thought of that. "Devon has arranged for her to stay at one of the Delrey mountain lodges, the one his ancestors used for hunting expeditions. They have taken steps to see that she does not return to Lorr."

I'd heard about those Delrey explorers and hunters. One of them had captured oversized winged reptiles that had been the models for the gliders that some of the wilder lads experimented with. If Selva Delrey was being held in those old quarters, she'd be out of the way for a very long time. I'd have given her a stint in the mines with the rest of the unsanctioned thieves and low-lifes, but private justice would have to do.

I took my coin and headed back to my digs, with a stop at the News Posts to see what was happening.

Post One had the bulletins from Admin. The Autocrat of Pangkot was terribly upset that one of his captains had been so stupid as to launch an attack on Lorr. He apologized profusely, and hoped the attempt would not disrupt the trade between Pangkot and Lorr. There was a detailed description of the battle, with special kudos for Captain Affrey Vikk and his Aerial Corps. They had dropped pots of flaming fish-oil on the Pangkoti ships while our naval vessels rammed them and turned the fleet around, scuttling back to Pangkot. So much for invaders from the south!

Post Two announced the formation of the Flatland Guards to supplement the Lorr City Guards, said Flatland Guards to be reinforced by some members of the Assassins' Guild.

Post Three had information about a Craftsman's Market in Flatlands, outside Guild authority, where Craftsmen could sell their products without having some Merchant acting as middleman, and people could buy them without having to pay the Merchant's overhead. Sounded like a good idea for everyone except the Merchants.

Post Four listed the results of several basher-bouts, and a new sporting event—the Pedishaw Dash! A contest between pedishaw drivers, organized by Aziz the Daredevil, who had done the run from Striver's Hill to the Waterfront in less than ten minutes. I had unleashed a monster when I let Aziz loose on the Grand Boulevard.

Post Five was devoted to eulogies for the beloved singer Liko Batom. I didn't bother to read them. He'd cut quite a swath through the female population of Lorr, and even a few males.

Of greatest interest was Post Six. There was plenty of speculation about the whereabouts of Selva Delrey, who had disappeared from Lorr's social scene after having made a reputation as a leading hostess and patron of the Arts. Guesses included a forthcoming infant (father assumed to be Ishka Kunine), a stint in the mines (due to association with aforesaid Ishka Kunine), or even banishment to one of the farthermost islands in the Southern Ocean.

And whether Kaisrin wanted publicity or not, the Vikk-Delrey split was already subject to public debate.

In short, Lorr was back to normal.

I stopped at Clothier's Alley to check my office. No one waiting for me, no messages. I left the coins I'd picked up at the Vikk mansion in the Clothier's Guild Bank, where they would be held for me under the sigil of Jake and Holly, and made my way back to my digs.

It was nearly sundown. Silver Moon was peeking over the horizon, Gold Moon would shortly be chasing it across the sky. I looked up and wondered if, somewhere out there, Old Earth was still rolling around its sun. Was it, as everyone feared, completely unlivable, destroyed by human greed and predation? Or had it reverted to its natural state, now that we were gone? Had the star called Sol exploded, engulfing all planets in its flames, or was it a dead star?

There was no way of knowing. We were alone on New Earth, and we had to make the best of it.

I gave up maundering, picked up my dinner order at Fletcher's, and went up to my rooms. It wasn't much, but it was my home, and I wasn't going to let Selva Delrey or Regina Polaris or anyone else remove me from it.

I checked the little cup where I'd carefully placed the tiny remnants of Ficus. I'd watered it, breathed on it, set it where the solar rays could reach it without burning it. I saw the tiny shoot, the merest speck of green.

Ficus lived! All was right with the City of Lorr!

UNTIL THE NEXT TIME…

ACKNOWLEDGMENTS

The first two sections of this book were written for a shared universe that never came to be: The World of Silver Moon. Thanks to John Betancourt and Carla Coupe, who released the stories back to me.

The song in "Prodigal Daughter" is based on "City of Doors" by Dr. Mary Crowell.

Thanks to Liz Burton, who read "A Private Matter" and decided to let me continue it.

ABOUT THE AUTHOR

ROBERTA ROGOW got her start writing for *Star Trek* fanzines in the mid-1970's. She mostly writes historical fiction, although she sometimes twists the history. Her most recent stories take place on a Manhattan Island that was settled by Spanish Moors instead of Dutch traders: *Last of the Mohegans* meets *The Thousand and One Nights*, with a Spanish accent.

Roberta retired from a 37-year career as a children's librarian in 2008. *Lorr and Disorder* is a return to her SF fanfic roots. She now lives in New Jersey, and spends her time going to science fiction and mystery conventions when she is not writing mysteries or singing filk (science fiction folk music).

ABOUT THE ARTIST

JENNIFER GIVNER of Acapella Design is a book cover artist and graphic designer with more than fifteen years' experience in cover design who has designed covers for both published authors and first-time writers. She illustrated the very first ebook coloring book, *Double Dip Penguin Surprise: The Coloring Book*, which was carried in Barnes and Noble's NY flagship store in 2000, along with the cover for the accompanying children's book, *Double Dip Penguin Surprise*. Her cover artwork has been showcased in a variety of media, including *Time* magazine, *Wired* magazine, on NPR, SiriusXM, WOAI radio, BlogTalkRadio, and in *Inside Sports Fishing* magazine.

In 2008, she designed the program and website for the stage play *A Breach of the Peace* starring Ed Asner. All proceeds from the performances benefited Habitat for Humanity of Greater Los Angeles.